The Red Dress

To the young men I grew up with:
Steven S., John Y., John F., George B., Wayne M., John R.,
Jamie C., Bruce C., Stewart M., and Ron G.

And to some of our teachers—good men in a bad time:
John B., Mark D., Hugh M., Alex L., Don G., Paul G., Tom W.,
Pat S., and Laurie V.

The Red Dress

One

One day last summer I went swimming at my health club on the outskirts of Peterborough. It's not a fancy place, but it has a little outdoor pool in the back—more for cooling down, I think, than for serious exercise. It was a relatively cool afternoon, and I was the only person in the water; there wasn't anyone on the deck, either. I had just swum a short distance underwater, and surfaced to see a rather squat man standing by the side of the pool, his head covered by a broad-brimmed tan hat. It took me aback a little, because I couldn't imagine how he'd got there in the five seconds I'd been below the surface.

"You're not paying attention," he said, beckoning to me. He looked very serious.

"I beg your pardon?" I said, more from surprise than because I hadn't heard him. At my health club, people don't talk to each other much. Most of us are there simply to exercise.

"You're not paying attention," he repeated—and then I heard

thunder in the distance, and a moment later everything suddenly went a brilliant, scalding white. I'd been hit by lightning, I found out later. I nearly died. It was very frightening.

But now I *am* paying attention, and part of my paying attention is telling a story that I've been pushing away for the last thirty years.

I grew up in Greenfield, a village of 2300 people about ten miles from the city of Peterborough in southern Ontario. Greenfield wasn't much to look at back in the mid-1970s. Most of its older downtown buildings had been replaced by new stores in the previous decade, and the outskirts were beginning to be taken over by the same suburban sprawl that hit pretty well everywhere else in Ontario around the same time. Many of the people who lived in and around Greenfield drove into Peterborough to work, and some got on the road in the early morning to make the eight o'clock shift at the auto plants in Oshawa.

I wish I could tell you I came from a happy, intact family, with a mom and dad and a younger sister and a dog or two—but I can't. My mom and dad split up when I was a baby, and I didn't see my dad after my fourth birthday. To be honest, I don't really remember him, and what I think I remember may be as much imagination as anything else—reconstructions from two faded photographs and a jacket he left behind. My mom, Barb, was a tough lady, so I'm not even sure I blame my dad for leaving: God knows, I nearly left several times in my teens, and I haven't so much as visited since the warm fall day I left for university back in 1976. But now I'm getting ahead of myself.

Barb and I lived in the two-storey apartment of an old house on Reid Street. The house had once been a large and gracious single-family home, but by the time we moved into it, it had been subdivided into three units. Our front door was at the back of the house, and you had to go round the side to get there. Barb wasn't much of a decorator, and I didn't know a paintbrush from a dust mop—not then—so the place was dark, drab, and dusty. It was home, though, the one home I'd ever known, and I only had books and television and the odd movie to tell me that family life could be very, very different.

Our street was quiet most of the time, but three doors down, on the other side, lived a single guy in his early thirties called Donny. I think he'd had a nervous breakdown at some point, and he very rarely came out of his house. *He* wasn't noisy, then, but an intense lady from Peterborough had taken him on as a kind of project. Every two or three days she'd drive out to Greenfield and try to get him out of the house. She'd bang and bang on his door, and when he didn't respond to the banging she'd begin calling out to him. "Donny, I know you're in there!" she'd yell. "It's time to get out of bed! We're going to the grocery store!" (Or, as the case might be, going for a walk, or going to a baseball game.) She'd keep this up for forty minutes at a time. Sometimes he'd come out and go with her, and sometimes he resolutely kept his door locked.

Sundays were the worst, because she was bound and determined Donny should accompany her to church. She'd arrive at 9:15 in the morning, and she would keep knocking and calling for well over an hour. "Donny! Church is at 11:00! We're going to church! The Lord is waiting for us. Don't keep the Lord waiting, Donny!" My mom called her the Christian Nazi. We had a couple of other interesting neighbours, and I may mention them later, but they don't figure prominently in this story.

The summer weekend that would change my life forever began normally enough. I'd grown into the habit of rising very early in the morning and going for long walks in the fields to the north of the village. I'm not even sure, now, why I went—what it was that got me up at the crack of dawn when many boys in the village were still sleeping off the beer they'd been drinking until a few hours before. It wasn't as though I had a destination in mind: I just walked. Anyway, on this particular day I had risen just after it was light and walked fast for a couple of miles through farmers' fields, then turned around and walked back. When I woke up I'd found a note from Barb with some money on the kitchen table. *Get me smokes*, she'd written, so I stopped at the corner store to buy her some cigarettes before I went home. She was at the kitchen table painting her nails when I came in.

Can I give you an objective picture of my mom? It's tough. She would have been about thirty-eight that summer, but her face looked older—probably because she'd spent a lot of time outdoors. She'd kept her figure, though, and was proud of it. Seen from a distance she could be mistaken for a woman in her twenties. She stood about five feet eight, so she was relatively tall, just a couple of inches shorter than I was, and she wore jeans most of the time. She smelled of cigarettes and a musky sort of perfume I didn't much like.

"Did you get me my smokes?" she said, by way of greeting. She'd glanced at me briefly when I came in; we weren't big on eye contact.

"Yup," I replied, and I went to the fridge for a glass of Kool-Aid. It was a little game: I should have just given them to her, but I liked getting her goat sometimes.

"Give 'em here," she said. I delayed another moment, but handed them over before she got wound. Winding Barb up was easy; unwinding her was a whole different matter. It wasn't worth it. She got mean.

"And the change," she said. I handed some over. "*All* the change." I should have known better: Barb knew to a penny what things cost.

"I need some for my lunch, Mom," I said. And this was true. I'd been making my own lunches for years.

"Make a sandwich."

"There's no bread."

"Make something else."

"There isn't anything else." The fridge was all but empty—a jar half-filled with jam and some wrapped cheese-food slices. A jug of Kool-Aid. Five bottles of beer.

"I'm doing the groceries tomorrow," she said. The tone of her voice told me she knew there wasn't anything to scrounge up.

"So can I keep a couple of bucks for today?" I asked, clutching the coins tightly in my pocket.

"Jesus!" she said. "All right. Go buy a loaf. Do something useful. I'm going out." She stood up, waving her nails in the air as she did so. It was a thing she did that I sort of liked: it was a girlish move, and it softened her, just for a moment.

"Will you be at Roger's?" I asked. Roger was her boyfriend. I knew she was going there. Of all her boyfriends over the years, he wasn't the worst. He had a job at the feed mill just off the main street, and he wasn't always drunk—just on weekends. But he had no time for me, and he liked Mom to go over to his place rather than to come to us.

"Maybe," said Barb, and she headed out, leaving a dirty coffee mug and the smell of a freshly lit cigarette behind her.

"Good-bye, Mom," I said. But she was gone.

I went out soon afterwards, retracing my steps to Staunton's Convenience just down the street. Mr. Staunton was in his late sixties, and had never liked teenagers. He watched me with narrowed eyes.

"You're back," he said, when I came in. He was a little man with a greasy comb-over and nicotine-stained fingers. If there was a Mrs. Staunton, I couldn't imagine how she put up with him.

"Yeah, I'm just getting a loaf of bread," I said.

"You shoulda got it before," he said, and his eyes followed me closely as I went down the bread aisle. How do people like that stay in business? Why did *I* keep going back? Force of habit? Lack of competition? I honestly don't know. Anyway, I chose a loaf of bread, then stopped to have a look at the magazine display before going up to the counter. I didn't dare take one down, though I really wanted a *Playboy* or *Penthouse*. I knew, however, that if I touched one, Mr. Staunton would insist that I buy it, and I didn't have nearly enough money.

When I put the loaf on the counter, Mr. Staunton asked: "This everything?"

"Yup," I said. It was your standard loaf of sliced white bread: that's what we ate in the seventies.

"You didn't swipe any candy, did you?" He sniffed, curling his lip as he did so.

"No, sir," I said. "I don't steal." I meant to sound firm and adult, but my voice betrayed me by cracking.

He sniffed again, then rang my purchase in. "Fifty-eight cents," he said. "Want a bag?"

"Yes, please." We used them for garbage. Proper garbage bags were expensive.

"I should charge extra for them bags," said Mr. Staunton, already regretting that he'd offered me one.

I came out of Staunton's Convenience a little faster than I should have, and nearly bowled over a middle-aged gentleman who was just going in. "Whoa, there, young fella!" he said. It was my high school history teacher.

"Mr. Boone!" I said. "I'm sorry, I wasn't looking."

I need to stop a moment and tell you a little about my high school, because knowing what kind of place it was will help frame this story. Champlain Secondary was a relatively new school—maybe just a decade old. It had been designed and built in the sixties, and as a result it was big and spread out and impersonal. There was a technical wing, given over to machine, wood, and auto shops, on one end, and at the opposite end there were two large gyms. In the middle were the academic classrooms, and the spaces where typing and home economics were taught, too. The front of the school looked neat enough, I guess, but the back had been taken over by a large smoking area, and this place was a no-go zone for teachers. This is where drug deals went down, and this is where kids came to fight. Some students smoked dope openly, and every Thursday a couple of bikers came roaring round the building to sell acid for the weekend. In the five years I attended Champlain, I saw fights back there every week, and sometimes knives were pulled. Once, I remember, when a gang was beating up a guy, three or four teachers came out, but the crowd wouldn't let them through, and they had to go back in and call the police and an ambulance. I'm only giving you a little piece of the picture here, but even at a remove of more than thirty years I find the hair rising on the back of my neck when I think about it.

Anyway, in a school where many teachers ran scared of students and had resolved simply to serve time until they could collect their pensions, Mr. Boone was a guy who still cared and still tried. He'd taught me modern European history the previous year, grade twelve (school went to grade thirteen in Ontario in those days), but he'd become so excited about the Renaissance that we spent the whole first term on it. I respected him, and I liked him.

"How are you, Charlie?" he asked. He was just a little guy—several inches shorter than me, with a mop of prematurely greying hair.

"I'm good. I'm fine," I said, grinning foolishly.

"How's your summer going?" He looked me in the eyes and waited to hear my answer. Most people I knew didn't do that.

"It's going great," I said. The sun was shining and the sky was a brilliant azure blue. For the moment, anyway, the summer did indeed feel wonderful.

"Are you working?" Mr. Boone's eyes were a sort of blue-grey, I discovered. He wasn't a handsome man, but he had kind eyes.

"No, not really. There's not much around here. I cut people's grass sometimes." In truth, there wasn't much work in Greenfield. If we'd had a car I might have been able to find something more interesting in Peterborough, but Barb had enough trouble finding money for rent without worrying about a car. And there was no bus between Greenfield and Peterborough: I don't know if there's one even now.

"Well, that's something," said Mr. Boone. "Are you coming back in the fall?'"

"You bet. I'm finishing high school," I said.

"And that's just the first step, isn't it?" he said—and in a place where many kids didn't trouble to do five years of secondary, that was a more remarkable thing for him to say than it sounds now. That was the thing about Mr. Boone: he made you think that maybe you were cut out for bigger things. Because he saw possibilities in you, you began to think they might be there, too.

"Yes. Yes, it is," I said, wondering if the conversation was over. I didn't want it to be, but I was scared of becoming one of those people who don't recognize when the other person wants to leave.

"Good lad," said Mr. Boone, smiling slightly. "Oh, did you see that Eddie Shack has retired?"

"Yes!" I said. Halfway through my grade twelve year we'd discovered we shared a fondness for the aging hockey player. He was a big, shambling fellow—not very skilled, maybe, but a real worker. "Boy, the Leafs are going to miss the Nose."

"He's a good guy," said Mr. Boone. "Lots of heart, old Eddie. I can still remember him playing with Cashman and Sanderson back in '67."

"Was that for the Bruins?" I asked. I was pretty sure it was, but I hadn't followed hockey closely when I was eight and nine. Barb used to make me go to bed before the game started.

"Yes, that was with the Bruins," said Mr. Boone. "And you know what happened the season before that?" He cocked his head and smiled.

"In '67?" I said. "The Leafs won the Stanley Cup!" That much I did know, even if I hadn't seen the series. The Leafs had been the talk of the playground that season.

"Glory days," said Mr. Boone, a faraway look in his eyes. "Let's hope they come around again soon." He was silent for a moment, then: "Well, I'm here to buy some milk, so I won't keep you, Charlie. Enjoy your summer."

"Yes, sir. You, too," I said, and embarrassed myself by reaching out for his hand. If he was embarrassed, though, he didn't show it, and we shook hands right there, right outside Staunton's Convenience, with Mr. Staunton glaring at us through the glass door.

"See you around, Charlie," said Mr. Boone. "Take care." And he was gone. I set out for home swinging my loaf of bread, and thinking, just for a moment, about what I might do the year after next.

Here's a little snapshot from my grade eleven year at Champlain Secondary—just to give you some sense of what it was like. I was one of a group that used to sit at the same long table every lunch to play euchre. There were thirteen or fourteen of us, but someone was always away for the day or off at some sort of practice, so there would be three games going for about forty minutes and no one was left out. We didn't take the games very seriously: it was just a fun thing. There were girls and guys together, and we played, and we talked and we joked.

At the start of grade twelve we were joined by a new girl, Lydia. She was blonde and pretty, and she wore fairly short skirts and partly transparent blouses, and it wasn't long before she paired off romantically with one of the guys from our euchre group. There wasn't a problem with that at first—except, perhaps, that some of us were a bit jealous—but after a week or so Herb stopped playing euchre. He and Lydia would sit off by themselves in another corner of the cafeteria. It seemed even more strange when eventually Herb stopped talking with any of us altogether. If we greeted him in the halls, he'd look the other way.

They broke up after six weeks or so—which was a pretty standard length for high school—and Lydia came back to the euchre table. Herb didn't. He slunk around the school looking low and demoralized, still declining to return the greetings of those among us who continued trying to make contact. But within a couple of weeks Lydia took up with another member of our informal euchre club, Brad, and the pattern repeated itself: lunch at another table, and Brad's sudden alienation from people who had previously been his good friends. And Brad had been one of the most enthusiastic and committed players.

When Lydia broke up with Brad, there was some talk at our table about what would happen next. Jen Hutchinson, who had been a good friend to both Herb and Brad, was particularly outspoken. "If she thinks she can come back and pick off the guys one by one, she's just plain wrong," she said. "That chick's gonna have to change her ways."

Someone asked her: "Why? What will you do?"

"Just you wait and see," Jen said. And she tapped her left palm with her right fist.

We didn't have long to wait. Three or four days after the breakup, Lydia went through the cafeteria line, then made her way over towards our table. She was just putting her tray down, when Jen spoke up: "You're not wanted here," she said.

"Says who?" said Lydia. She didn't look in the least intimidated.

"I say so," said Jen, getting to her feet. She was a well-built girl—*robust* is the word Mr. Boone might have used. I wouldn't have wanted her angry with me.

"Cat fight," said someone gleefully behind me—at another table. The cafeteria suddenly hushed.

"What are you going to do about it?" said Lydia. She was ominously calm.

"Why don't we go outside and discuss it?" said Jen.

"Why don't you go fuck yourself?" said Lydia—and she suddenly picked up the cup of coffee from her tray and threw it in Jen's face.

The fight wasn't even close. Jen was the bigger girl, but there was a viciousness about Lydia that took your breath away. She jumped the table and had Jen on the floor before anyone could move. It took several of us to haul her off and away—and she was able to get in a well-aimed kick to Jen's head before we did.

But at least Lydia did not come back to the table again. And after a couple of weeks she took up with a boy in grade thirteen, and it was clear that she had moved on socially.

A month later Herb returned to the euchre table, his tail between his legs. A week after that Brad came back, too. And the rest of us eventually learned that Lydia had done the same thing with each of them: she'd got them fairly besotted with her, then persuaded them that the rest of us were routinely saying ugly things about them, and that she, Lydia, was really the only friend they had.

It's amazing what damage focused malevolence can do.

I was about halfway home from Staunton's Convenience, turning off Concession and onto Reid, when I heard a voice behind me. "Charlie! Wait up." It was my friend Randy.

Were we friends? We shared space. During my high-school years we saw each other, and talked, every day. He was as short as Mr. Boone, maybe five feet six, but he had dark greasy hair and a bad case of acne on his chin and cheeks. He always wore a black T-shirt, and usually kept it on a day longer than he should have. But most of us did in those days.

"Wanna go halves on a two-four this weekend?" he asked me. We'd resumed walking.

"Nah," I said. It wasn't the first time he'd made the suggestion, and I'd never bought in. I was surprised he kept asking.

"Why not?"

"I'm trying to save some money," I said. A half-truth. I knew I should be saving, but I hadn't yet begun.

"What for?" asked Randy. He turned his head a little and spat on the sidewalk.

"You never know." I shrugged, and hoped I sounded mysterious. My grass-cutting money, kept in my bedroom chest of drawers, was pretty well depleted a couple of days after I made it. I liked to buy newspapers and chocolate bars, and on those rare occasions that I went to Peterborough, I visited a second-hand bookstore on Water Street. Besides, seeing what beer did to Barb's various boyfriends had made me wary of it.

"Don't come to me beggin' for beer Saturday night," said Randy, twisting up his face. He wasn't good-looking at the best of times, and this expression didn't help.

"Have I ever?" I'd never done that. He knew I'd never done that.

"Once or twice." A flat lie—and a strange one. Either that, or he was confusing me with someone else from school.

"I have not!" I said, sounding much younger than I wanted to. But Randy had already moved on.

"Jake and me were thinkin' of shootin' some pool tonight," he said.

"At Grampy's?" I looked sideways at him.

"Yeah. Wanna come?"

"Maybe," I said. "Yeah." I didn't often do stuff like that. Truth is, I didn't get out much at all.

Saturday night at Grampy's was a world all of its own. You wouldn't think a place as small as Greenfield could support a pool hall, and looking back now I wonder what dubious enterprises Grampy had his fingers in. Yes, he got a certain number of people driving out from Peterborough to play—truckers, labourers, a few college boys—but the place was usually pretty quiet. At the best of times, and a summer's Saturday night was peak season, three of the five tables would be in use, and there'd be a knot of people at the bar drinking and smoking.

I went through the door, nodded at Grampy—a pot-bellied guy in his late fifties with a lit cigarette dangling from his lip—and went over to where Randy and Jake were playing. If Randy was my friend, then Jake was simply someone I knew. At twenty, he was three years older than Randy and me, and he'd dropped out of Champlain in grade ten. I don't know how he supported himself, but I suspect welfare provided his chief income, supplemented by the odd unofficial labouring job. Randy told me he had a kid with a girl in Peterborough, but he certainly didn't live with them. He was skinny—skinny and tall—and he wore black cowboy boots.

"Hi," said Randy. He was leaning on his cue, and he nodded at me.

"Hi," I said. I watched Jake make a shot. "You playing Boston?" I asked. I didn't know much about pool.

"Guy's a fuckin' genius," said Jake, not even bothering to look at me.

"Would you get me a Coke, Charlie?" asked Randy. The question surprised me with its delicacy. Jake was obviously not doing too well, and Randy thought I should step away for a moment, but he didn't ask for a beer (which would have taken half of what I had in my pocket).

"Sure," I said, and I turned to Jake, hoping to make things better. "Would you like—" I began. Jake scratched his shot.

"Don't talk when I'm takin' a fuckin' shot!" he erupted.

"Okay, I'm sorry, I was just—"

"Don't ever fuckin' talk to me when I'm fuckin' takin' a fuckin' shot!" said Jake, and he advanced on me a couple of steps. His eyes were bloodshot and his cheeks were flushed.

"Okay," I said, backing up. "Sorry. I was just offering to get you—"

"What are you, a fuckin' waitress, or somethin'?" said Jake, and that was my cue to go. Profanity from guys like Jake was just part of the landscape and, God knows, I was used to hearing it. But when he questioned my sexuality—and that's where he was heading, I knew—it was time to go.

"See you later, Randy," I said, continuing to back away. Jake wasn't the kind of guy you turned your back on.

"Ah, no, Charlie, don't go yet," said Randy. (I don't know: maybe we were friends. Or maybe he just didn't want to be left alone with Jake.)

"Let the fuckin' pussy go," said Jake. "I'm takin' that shot over again." I moved away from the table and headed back towards the door.

"Hey!" shouted Grampy from behind the bar. "You boys keep the fuckin' noise down over there!"

What did I do after that? I went home and watched television. Barb was obviously staying over with Roger, so I could choose the channel, and I didn't have to put up with her commentary on the shows. After that I made myself a sandwich and went to bed, and did what every other unattached male of seventeen did when I got there. I kept a couple of old skin magazine between the mattress and the box springs.

Didn't I have other friends? A few. I knew a lot of people: you couldn't help meeting people in a high school with about a thousand kids. It was complicated, though. Most of those kids were bused long distances—or what then seemed like long distances—to school, and if you didn't have a car yourself, you had to rely on your parents to drive you. I really liked some people, girls and guys, from farms in the outlying areas. We ate lunch together and, as I've said, played euchre in the school cafeteria. But farm kids had chores after school and on weekends, so socializing with them any time other than Saturday night was difficult. As for Saturday night, the fact that we didn't have a car, and the fact that I was embarrassed to invite people home, made it difficult. There was a girl I'd had a serious crush on in grade eleven, Marilyn, but her mom met my mom in the Food Mart about two weeks after we started going steady, and that finished that. And male friends? Most of the guys in the village were like Randy, and one Randy was enough.

So that was Saturday night. On Sunday morning, I woke up at 6:00 and couldn't go back to sleep, so I went for my usual walk. West along Reid, up Concession, along Coyle, across the railroad tracks, then out to the fields to the north. And it felt good. The sun was shining, the sky was a pale blue, there were birds singing. It was possible to imagine a world without Jakes, without smoky pool halls—a world where mothers came home nights, and there was decent food in the fridge, and beautiful naked girls and women frolicked in fields just like the ones I was walking through. I was seventeen. I have to think that it was partly sexual energy that sent me out into these fields in the early morning.

But it wasn't a naked woman that I met in those farmers' fields. Off in the distance I spied, some moments before we met, a slim, nicely dressed man in his early forties. He was walking towards me, on the same path I was taking, and something about the way he carried himself—the easy way he swung his arms, his sure-footedness, his obvious fitness—told me that he wasn't ordinary, he wasn't average. He wasn't the kind of guy, certainly, that Barb could ever hope to bring home. We met in the middle of a field, and he smiled at me.

"Good morning," he said, stopping. He was clean-shaven, I saw, and wearing a sports jacket. He had on a subtle cologne or after-shave. It wasn't Old Spice.

"Hi," I said, a little shyly. His eyes were blue and piercing, and I looked down at my feet.

"Just out for a walk?"

"Yes." I was inexplicably tongue-tied. I'd been much more forth-coming with Mr. Boone—but then I knew him.

"It's a fine day," he said, and he slipped his hand into the breast pocket of his jacket, withdrawing a silver cigarette case.

"Yes," I agreed. My eye was caught by the flash of silver.

"Cigarette?" He opened the case and offered me one. There were twenty of them, and even unlit they smelled rich and exotic.

"No. No, thank you," I said. It was the first time an adult had offered me a smoke. It made me feel grown-up.

He smiled. He wasn't offended. "Well, you're quite right," he said. "Not a good habit. My one great vice."

"My mom smokes," I said, feeling I should say something else. "It sort of put me off it. The house stinks. It's fine doing it outside," I added hastily, as he lit up.

"You're a wise young man," he said, exhaling. "My wife makes me do all my smoking outside." He surveyed the fields with a smile—the smile of a man utterly at ease with himself. "Not that that's any hardship on a day like this one."

"Do you live around here?" I asked. I hadn't seen him before. I'd have remembered him if I had.

"Yes. Not far. We live on Hazelwood."

"Hazelwood Estates?" I asked. Hazelwood Estates was the ritzy suburb to the northwest of the village. The homes were huge, and they had sprawling back yards. Randy said that about half of them had swimming pools. Roger had told my mom that his brother, a plumber's assistant, had helped install brass fixtures in many of the bathrooms. And a few of them had bidets, he'd said. ("What's a bi-det?" I'd asked. "Don't ask stupid questions," Barb had said. I don't think she knew either.)

The man laughed. "That's what the developer calls them, yes," he said. "It makes them sound much too grand for my taste."

"They're incredible houses!" I said. "Do you have a pool?" Having a pool defined wealth for me: swimming was one of my favourite things in the world. I'd have spent the whole summer in the water if I could get away with it.

"Yes, we have a pool. And a beautiful, Japanese-style garden. My wife's work."

"Is she a gardener?" I asked. I'd planted some marigolds once in a window box. They hadn't come to much.

"I think I should probably call her a garden *designer* rather than a gardener," he said, thinking about my question carefully. "She makes drawings of how things should look, and then she hires other people to do most of the physical work."

"She's a landscape architect, then," I said proudly. It was a job category I'd learned about in the last year. I liked to show off my little tidbits of knowledge when I had a chance.

"That's right," he said. "Now, how would you know about that sort of thing?"

"It's what I'd like to do, maybe. When I've finished college. Mr. Boone suggested it."

"And who is Mr. Boone?" He was still looking directly at me, but I found I could now meet his gaze. He was boyishly handsome, with dark brown hair, well-defined eyebrows, full lips, and a strong jaw. Only the laugh lines around his eyes gave his age away.

"He's my history teacher," I said— "Or he was. I've moved on now. I'm going into grade thirteen." I was telling him more than I needed to, but he seemed interested. He was listening carefully. In fact, he listened just as carefully as Mr. Boone himself.

"Was he a good history teacher?"

"Yes," I said. "He was great. He really was. He taught us all about the Renaissance. He was supposed to be teaching about the French Revolution and the American Revolution and the Industrial Revolution, but he got really excited about the Renaissance. I know a lot about it."

"Do you?" he said, nodding thoughtfully. "Do you?" He wasn't mocking me. And then: "A great teacher is very precious."

"Yeah. That's true," I said. And I still believe that, these many years later, still believe that a good teacher can make a huge difference in a young person's life.

"My name is Serge," he said, offering me his hand. "Serge Boorman." His handshake was firm, not aggressive. He didn't try to crush my fingers. I introduced myself. "And do you often walk across these fields?" he asked.

"When I've got something to think through, yeah," I said. I didn't say that I felt driven to it by a restlessness in my body and mind.

"You find walking helps you to think?" Again, his eyes engaged mine. He was interested in what I had to say.

"Yeah," I said. "I do."

"I find that, too," said Serge. "I do some of my best thinking on walks like this one." He took a deep draw on his cigarette, held the smoke in for a moment, then let it slip silkily from his nostrils. Barb's boyfriends didn't smoke like that.

"What kinds of things do you think about?" I asked.

"Oh, where to travel next. How to get in touch with old friends. What birthday gift I might buy Selina. Selina is my wife."

"Is it her birthday soon?"

"This Friday," said Serge. He looked thoughtful.

"How old will she be?" I asked. I didn't know any better. I really didn't.

Serge laughed. "Now that would be telling! But she's a good many years younger than I am." He sucked smoke into his lungs again, and his eyes scanned the sky, taking in the sight of two hawks circling high above us. They were especially active that summer. "We humans were meant to be walkers," he said, his eyes meeting mine again. "Our ancestors followed the wild animals, you know, and later they took their herds on great annual migrations. Walking is our natural condition."

"I guess so," I said. This was a new idea to me. I would need to think about it.

"They made camp whenever they rested," he said. "And they travelled light. They weren't caught up in their possessions. And because they walked so much, they were very fit. There was no obesity."

I said nothing, but I nodded. It made sense.

Serge had reached some kind of decision. He dropped his cigarette, and ground it out carefully with his foot. "You must visit us, Charlie," he said. "Selina is always delighted to show off her garden."

"Do you mean it?" I asked, stunned at the idea. In my experience, adults did not invite teenagers to their homes. Teenagers were, at best, encumbrances—at worst, life-wrecking mistakes. (Barb had called me some choice names when she was drunk, including, memorably, *Parasite Boy.*)

"Of course I mean it," said Serge. "You'll find us at 84 Hazelwood. Come tomorrow afternoon. Have coffee with us. Or do you not drink coffee?"

"I love coffee!" I said. I didn't often drink it, but when I had some extra change I'd buy a cup in the school cafeteria. Some of my friends drank gallons of the stuff.

"Splendid. We'll have coffee and cake."

"Should I bring my swimsuit?" I asked. (And yes, I cringe at the memory, but I have so many worse things to cringe over.)

Serge just laughed again. "Yes," he said. "Bring your swimsuit."

"Okay, then. I will," I said, still half expecting him to reveal he hadn't been serious, it was all a great big joke at my expense.

"Good," he said. "Until tomorrow, then, Charlie. Good-bye." And he set off towards Greenfield, and I continued on, through the fields and into the forest beyond, marvelling still, marvelling, at this change in my fortunes.

Two

I'd recently overheard Barb talking about me with Roger. They were downstairs, in the living room. They'd just turned off the television, and Barb had gone out to the kitchen to fetch two beers. I'd come in while they were watching *Kojak*, and it was turned up so loud they hadn't heard me. I was up in my bedroom with the door open.

"I'm worried about that kid of mine," said Barb. I could hear a sharp intake of breath as she took her first puff of a new cigarette.

"What's wrong with him?" asked Roger. I was scarcely on his radar screen.

"No ambition." The couch springs groaned as she settled back down beside him. It had been second- or third-hand when she'd bought it years before.

"So kick him out," said Roger. And he burped. A long one. That's the kind of guy Roger was—always burping and farting.

"He's my kid." Barb's voice was flat.

"So?" Roger didn't have children.

"So, he's got nowhere else to go," she said. "His dad wouldn't do nothin' for him." I wondered if this was true. I wondered if my dad knew anything about me. The last I'd heard of him he'd struck out for the Yukon, lured, perhaps, by the dream of finding gold. I could picture him beside a fire up there, his tent behind him, a loyal dog at his side, the stars twinkling overhead. Sometimes I wished I could be there, too.

"Is he goin' back to school in September?" asked Roger.

"Yeah." Another sharp intake of smoke. I could imagine the look on her face as she sucked it in and held it there for a moment. Smoking didn't seem to bring Barb much pleasure: it was just something she did.

"Then he can collect student pogey and move out on his own." There was always a rasp in Roger's voice—the legacy of thirty years of Camels.

"I dunno," said Barb. There was a silence. "Hey, remind me, will ya," she said. "The welfare lady's coming at 11:00 tomorrow."

This overheard conversation was playing in my head when I returned home from the fields Sunday morning. It wasn't yet 9:00, so Barb wasn't home from Roger's. She might not be back for hours. I made myself some breakfast and ate it, then stood at the kitchen window watching a robin feed her young in a nest under the drainpipe on the back of the house. There must have been a rich supply of grubs not far away, because she was never gone for long, and as soon as the chicks heard her, or thought they'd heard her, their little heads came into view again, their beaks wide open. After a few minutes, I heard the front door open, and a moment later Barb came into the kitchen. She immediately began to make coffee.

"Hi, Mom," I said, after watching her plug in the kettle. She drank instant coffee, spooning it into a large mug stamped with the words BIKER CHICK and a picture of a tough-looking hen on a motorcycle, the bird sporting tattoos and an old-fashioned German army helmet.

Barb grunted. Then: "Did you get that bread?"

"Yeah," I said. "I had toast this morning. The loaf's in the cupboard."

"Where did you go?" she asked. "I called."

"You did?" I said. It didn't seem likely. "I went for a walk."

"He went for a walk," she echoed mockingly, addressing an imaginary audience. "What for?"

"Just for the exercise," I said. "I met somebody."

"A girl?" asked Barb, instantly alert. I didn't know how to understand her views about my friendships with girls. She had a very low opinion of my status most of the time, but seemed to believe that some tramp was determined to seduce me at the first opportunity and force me to support her and our baby for the rest of my miserable life. It occurred to me a few years ago that maybe that's what she tried to do with my dad.

"No. A man," I said. "A nice guy. He offered me a cigarette." A memory of Serge's silver cigarette case flashed in my mind.

"Did you take it?" Hard. Sharp. Suspicious. She didn't want me to smoke. I think she figured I might start stealing hers.

"No," I said.

"What did he want?" she asked.

"Just to talk." I paused. "He invited me round for coffee."

"He did what?" said Barb. She was rummaging around in the cupboard looking for the artificial sweetener. If she didn't find it quickly, she'd accuse me of hiding it from her.

"He invited me round for coffee tomorrow," I repeated.

Barb looked at me for the first time that morning. "I don't want you visiting with no fags," she said. Her hair was, as ever, carefully styled, but there was a metallic harshness to the colour: it wasn't quite true.

This took me aback. "He's not a fag, Mom: he's married. He invited me round for coffee and a swim and to see his garden."

Barb had found the sweetener and was now making herself some toast. "Where does he live?" she asked.

"Hazelwood Estates." I knew the name would impress her, whatever she might say.

"He's rich, then."

"I guess so," I said. A flicker of movement caught my eye, and I saw that the mother robin had returned to the nest, her beak full of grubs. Her babies were desperate to be fed—frantic with hunger.

Barb took the jam out of the fridge, and brought it down on the table with a bang. "I don't want you going," she said. She had a way of narrowing her lips and knitting her brows when she was angry.

"Why not?"

"What's his name?"

"Serge. Why don't you want me going?"

She opened the jam and got a knife from the drawer. "Did you see his wife?" Her lips were almost white. I felt the stirrings of rebellion.

"No. She was at home."

"He's a fag," she said. "Trust me. They all say they're married, but when you show up they want to play hide-the-weenie." She spoke as if she'd had wide experience with wealthy homosexuals.

"He had a wedding ring," I objected. I wasn't sure it was a wedding ring, but there had certainly been a gold ring on one of his hands.

"What?" said Barb. She was trying to extricate the toast from the toaster. It was an old machine, and often reluctant to give up its contents.

"He had a wedding ring," I said. "On his finger."

"It doesn't mean anything," she said, unplugging the toaster and turning it upside down.

"It does to some people. And he talked about his wife as if he really loved her." And this at least was absolutely true.

Barb turned to me again, and looked at me scornfully. "Oh, well, that's sweet," she said. "Deep cover. She's probably out of town. If she exists."

I decided to take a stand. "He's a nice guy," I said. "I'm going." I wasn't entirely without backbone, but my voice shook a little, and I had to clench my fists to keep from trembling.

"Go, then," said Barb. "See if I care. But don't come whining to me if he makes a grab for your ass."

"Why do you have to make everything so cheap?" I asked. But the conversation was over.

So on Monday afternoon I made my way to the Boormans, taking much the same route I took when I went walking in the fields, but going a little further to the west. It was a pleasant walk, made all the nicer when I saw, in a large vacant lot, eleven or twelve Canada Geese sunning themselves in the grass. It wasn't clear to me why they were there: they were some distance from the water, and I wouldn't have thought that the scrub grass provided them with much to eat, but they seemed perfectly happy. I stopped to admire them for a moment or two: they all had black heads and necks, but with a white band just below the eyes that looked a little like a chinstrap. They didn't seem much bothered by my presence, simply honking quietly among themselves: it was as if they knew I meant them no harm. Eventually, well content, I moved on, and soon found myself in Serge's neighbourhood.

There were no sidewalks in Hazelwood Estates: I guess the developers assumed that everyone had at least two cars. I had to walk on the road, then, and it was a fair hike between driveways—at least compared to the thirty feet or so between driveways in the village itself. God only knows how the numbering system worked, because there were nowhere near 84 houses on the subdivision. The Boormans' was easy to find, though: theirs was the seventh house in from county road 2, and I soon found myself walking up a newly paved driveway lined with saplings. The house itself was probably twice the size of the house we lived in, three apartments and all, and was framed by newly planted trees, shrubs, and flowers. It was what I've since learned to call a mock Tudor design, with half-timbering and elaborate decorations.

I rang the doorbell, and heard a musical chime deep in the house. While I waited, I looked at the flowerbeds near the front door: there were several different kinds of flowers (dianthus, poppies, foxgloves), but they were all in shades of red. I'd never seen anyone do that before.

A moment passed, and the door opened almost soundlessly. There, framed in the entrance, was a pretty young Asian woman. I guessed then that she was Chinese, but later learned that she was from the Philippines. (We were only just beginning to see non-white people in rural Ontario.) She was in her early twenties, with jet-black hair and very pale skin. She wore a modest blue dress, and no make-up.

"Hi, Mrs. Boorman. I'm Charlie," I said. "Serge invited me." It felt good to say *Serge*.

"Hello, Mr. Charlie," said the Asian lady. "But I am not Mrs. Boorman. I work for her." She smelled of soap, as though she'd just scrubbed herself clean.

"What's your name, then?" I asked, surprised. I hadn't expected anyone apart from one or other of the Boormans.

"I am Milly," she replied. "Please come in." As she opened the door a little wider she seemed almost to bow me in.

I stepped into the front hall. It was a little dark after the July sunshine, but some light spilled through a small window onto a vase of red peonies on a table just inside the door. I noticed fleetingly that there was a tiny ant on one of the fragrant blossoms.

"Is Serge here?" I asked.

"Mr. Boorman has not come back yet, but Mrs. Boorman is expecting you," said Milly. She had an oddly formal way of speaking. Her English was perfect, but she used no contractions.

At that instant Selina, Serge's wife, came into the front hall—and my heart all but stopped. She was a stunningly beautiful woman. Or was she? I honestly don't know for sure. I know that my first response to her was that she was beautiful, but I've got to factor in my relative isolation from sophisticated, elegant people. She was slim, as was her husband; she was blonde; she'd applied makeup so skilfully you had to look carefully to see that she had any on; and a light floral scent preceded her. She was wearing a white cotton summer dress that contrasted wonderfully with her tan. She was in her early thirties, but she looked as fresh as any eighteen-year-old I'd ever met. Yes, she was beautiful.

"Thank you, Milly," she said. "Good afternoon, Charlie." She offered me her hand, and I took it. It was soft and cool and I wanted to crush my lips against her fingers.

"Hi," I said, ducking my head a little.

"It's lovely to meet you," she said. "My husband is detained, but he shouldn't be long. He told me you share my passion for gardens." She was smiling, but it was a friendly, welcoming smile without the slightest hint of condescension. If ever eyes sparkled, hers did.

"Yes. Yes, I do," I said, fumbling for words. Until that moment I would not have described my fondness for trees and shrubs and flowers as a *passion*, but it was immediately clear to me that that's what it was.

"May I show you mine?" Selina asked. I've wondered many times, over these last many years, whether there was a deliberate sexual dimension to some of the things she said to me. Was she being consciously seductive? Did she intuit my desire, my *other* passion, and play to it? Again, I don't know. There are so many things I'm just not sure about. What I do know, without doubt, is that my heart fluttered as I gazed at her.

"Yes. Please," I said.

"Milly will take ... is it a towel?" she said, noticing the rolled-up towel I carried in my left hand. I was wearing my swimsuit under my shorts.

"Yes. These are my swimming things," I said. "For in case we go swimming," I added unnecessarily. And that sounded irredeemably goofy even to my ears.

Selina laughed—but it was a kind laugh. "And we may well, after you've seen the garden and had some coffee and a chat." And then, her tone changing slightly: "Could you serve in ten minutes, please, Milly?"

"What if Mr. Boorman isn't here, ma'am?" said Milly.

The faintest trace of annoyance flickered over Selina's face—not so much with Serge, I sensed, as with Milly for asking the question. "Oh, serve anyway," she said. "He can join us on the second cup." Her lip, which had curled slightly, resumed its normal position, but I'd had a fleeting glimpse of impatience.

"Yes, ma'am," said Milly. And she turned and left us, taking away my towel, and leaving me to enjoy the full radiance of Selina's presence.

"Is she like a servant?" I asked awkwardly.

"I suppose she is, in a way—but I think of her more as a member of the family," said Selina. "Come," and she led me down the long hall and into a gorgeous living room replete with leather couches and walnut end tables and antique lamps. I paused briefly to admire the opulence, but Selina moved on, her hips undulating slightly, and so I followed, as I have followed many a pair of undulating hips since, though never again with the same mute hunger and dog-like admiration.

And where did she lead? She led me through French doors into another world. If the house was the most palatial I'd ever entered—and it was—the garden was like a fantasy, a dream. Now, I might not have met many sophisticated, elegant ladies before, but there were certainly some fine gardens in Greenfield. They tended to be of the English country garden style: meandering paths and beds filled with flowers, shorter ones at the front and taller ones near the back. Rose gardens, too, were popular, and done well, in the village. But this ... Selina's garden would, I'm sure, have passed muster even in Kyoto.

Directly outside the French doors there was a tiny lawn, and that lawn swiftly defined itself as the bank of a pond that, because it circled the garden, looked like a stream. You crossed the pond via a stone bridge—a piece of rock that resembled nothing so much as those stone plinths you see in Europe, but laid horizontally above the water. That took you to an island in the middle of the pond; an island built up, I'd guess, by a large earthen deposit, and covered in boulders, berry-laden bushes, ferns, and dwarf trees. We crossed the stone bridge and wandered over the small island, Selina pointing out features of which she was particularly proud. I said nothing for several moments, but simply drank in what she was showing me.

Selina eventually paused, and looked at me with a half-smile. "Do you like it?" she asked.

"It's beautiful. It's amazing," I said. "I've never seen anything like it."

"Oh, I'm so glad," said Selina, touching my arm lightly. (I thrilled at her touch.) "I designed it, this winter, even before we moved in, and it was only finished a few weeks ago. Not that a garden is ever really finished."

"The trees weren't here?" I asked, incredulous. Several of them were taller than I was.

"No, I had to begin from scratch," said Selina. "A blank slate. Shall we head back?"

We began to retrace our steps back towards the bridge. "I've seen lots of gardens in town," I said, "but this ... this is amazing." And it was. It was like nothing I'd ever seen before in Greenfield, or anywhere else. There was a vision at work there, an aesthetic sense, that I could admire, but not properly understand. It was beautiful, yes—but it was also somehow alien.

"You're so sweet," said Selina. And, stepping off the gravel path, she drew me over towards a stone lantern. "This is from the Edo era. It was a present from Serge."

"An early birthday present?" I asked.

"No—a Christmas present. I have no idea what he's got me for my birthday. Do you know?" Her laughing eyes locked with mine for a moment.

I dropped my gaze. "No, I don't," I said. "He was still thinking about it when I met him on the walk." (*And what a lucky man to have such challenges*, I thought.)

"I think he's late because he's gone to fetch whatever it is," said Selina. "I'm so excited. He always knows exactly what gift to give. What's the best present you've ever received?"

"I don't know," I said. "I got a bike once. It was second-hand, but it was pretty good." A mental image of it presented itself unbidden: it was a red three-speed with high handlebars and a banana-style seat. I'd ridden it for years—until it had been stolen from just outside our front door.

"Was it from your parents?" Selina asked.

"It was from my mom. Or she said it was," I said. I quietly suspected it came from a service club. "I don't know my dad."

"Oh, I'm sorry," said Selina. "I didn't mean to hurt you—"

"You haven't hurt me," I said. "I'm fine." (*You could always kiss me*, I thought. *That would make it better.*)

"A bike is a wonderful present," said Selina. "I rode mine every day when I was young."

"You're still young," I objected. Saying so, of course, gave me licence to look at her carefully, and I did so, trying to pretend that I was appraising her objectively. That she was slim, blonde, and tanned I've already mentioned; what I can't begin to convey is how radiant she was in that instant. It was as if she herself gave off light and energy.

"I'm going to be thirty-two on Friday," she said. "I'm beginning to feel middle-aged."

"You look like you're in your twenties," I said. "I'm serious." And I was.

"You can come again any time," said Selina, laughing. We had reached the stone bridge, and she turned, briefly, and surveyed the island, then looked forward to the house. "I'm a lucky lady," she said.

I stared at her. I could not speak. She was completely in the sun, and the light was bright and direct enough that I could see the contours of her perfect body through her white dress. I had discovered a few moments before, when the sun caught her in a certain way, that she was wearing the skimpiest of undergarments, but it was her face that held me now—her blonde hair, her green eyes, her red, red lips.

After a moment, she became aware of my scrutiny, and smiled brilliantly at me. "Let's go and see about coffee, shall we?" she said, and she took my hand and led me back across the bridge, through the French doors, and into her opulent living room. Her home was everything that mine was not.

The lady from the welfare office visited about once every three months. I tried not to be there when she came by, but we never knew exactly when she would come so, inevitably, I was sometimes there. Barb would invite her into the kitchen and sit stiffly on one side of the table, chain-smoking, while the welfare lady asked her routine questions. I'd been upstairs in my room, with the door open, during the June visit.

"I'm sorry to be late," the welfare lady had said. She was middle-aged, a little overweight, and had rather a brisk manner.

"It's okay," said Barb. "I did some cleaning while I waited."

I heard a file being opened. "Now. Is your son still at home, Ms. Knowles?" (*Ms.* Knowles, if you please. The welfare lady was a feminist. Barb hated her.)

"Yeah," said Barb. "He'll be goin' back to the high school in the fall."

Even upstairs I could hear the welfare lady's pen scratching as she made her notes. "And is he the only other person living in the house?" That was the loaded question: if there was, of course, and if that person was a wage-earning male, Barb might no longer be eligible for social assistance.

"Yup." Barb took a deep draw on her cigarette, and blew the smoke out, I was sure, just a little to the side: close enough to the welfare lady to irritate her, but not so close that the act could be seen as aggressive.

So we re-entered Selina's living room, and I blinked a few times as my eyes adjusted to the different quality of light. Selina invited me to sit, and I chose a plush armchair and settled into it with a sense of astonishment that any chair could be so comfortable. We chatted for a moment or two about inconsequential things—or things that I don't remember now, anyway—then Milly came in with coffee, cake, and three cups on a small trolley.

"Shall I serve, ma'am?" she asked. She didn't look directly at Selina.

"Yes, please, Milly. How do you take your coffee, Charlie?" And so the coffee-serving ritual unfolded—the beverage poured from a silver percolator, frothed with cream, and sweetened with candy sugar. This marked the first time in my seventeen years on earth that I'd ever drunk real coffee, or taken any beverage from a china cup. It was surely a day of firsts.

"Mr. Boorman is home, ma'am," said Milly, as she poured a third cup, clearly for Serge.

"Oh, good. Was he carrying a package of any kind, Milly?" asked Selina.

"I did not notice that he had—" Milly began, but at that instant Serge came into the room.

"Now, don't interrogate Milly, my darling. I purposely came in through the side entrance so that neither of you would see me." He bent to kiss Selina, and her lips met his. (I felt an electric jolt of jealousy.) "I'm glad to see our new friend has been taken care of. What do you think of the garden, Charlie?"

"It's amazing," I said. "It's like a fairy land." I wondered, briefly, if the word *fairy* was a mistake, but it clearly wasn't an issue at all.

"There," Serge said, turning to Selina: "I told you Charlie was a young man of discriminating taste." His hand lingered on her shoulder, his manicured fingers gently caressing her.

"He's been very sweet," said Selina. "Look, Milly's poured coffee for all of us. Sit down and join us."

"I will," said Serge, and he sat down beside her on the couch. "We want to know about your teachers and your school, Charlie," he said. "We should really get to know each other."

And they did get to know me. They asked me questions, and they listened to my answers, and they laughed when I told jokes. And a full hour passed magically, at least for me: I'd never been *heard* like that before. I'd never before had the undivided attention of two bright, handsome adults ... and I basked in it. Towards the end of that first coffee, I remember, Serge and Selina were laughing at a silly story I told them about a noise I could make in my throat—a noise I sometimes deployed in the classroom to annoy a teacher I didn't much like.

"And he couldn't tell where it was coming from?" asked Serge, smiling broadly.

"He had no idea!" I said. "I was making the noise in my throat—but he couldn't tell!" I produced the sound for them: it sounded like nothing so much as a hungry guinea pig.

"But did he get angry?" asked Selina, clearly concerned that I might have found myself in trouble.

"I think he was surprised more than anything else," I said, and I stopped laughing as I remembered the bewildered look on Mr. Jacob's face. It had been a stupid thing to do, I realized. He was a heavy man with a triple chin and eczema on his elbows, but there was no malevolence in him. I was suddenly taken aback by my own unkindness.

"Well!" said Selina, smiling again. "Oh, Serge, is there time for a quick swim before we go out?"

"*Are* you going out?" I asked, crestfallen. I didn't want the visit to end.

"We have reservations for dinner, Charlie," said Serge. "In Oshawa. There's a little French restaurant we're fond of there. But yes," he said, turning back to Selina, "I think there's time for a quick swim."

Selina rose. "Will you gentlemen excuse me?" she said.

"Aren't you going to swim?" I asked, dismayed at the thought that I might lose her company.

"Yes, of course," said Selina. "I'm just going to get changed." Her lips parted slightly, and she pushed her hair away from her face.

"Oh. Where should I change?" I asked.

"I'll send Milly to take you somewhere," said Selina. "See you out there." And she slipped away, leaving behind the traces of her fragrance—floral, yes, but also cinnamon and orange.

Serge took the opportunity of Selina's leaving to take out his cigarette case. "Well, this has been very pleasant, Charlie," he said. "Selina and I don't see many people, so your company is particularly welcome."

"How come you don't see many people?" I asked. I imagined

that they must have scores and scores of friends—artists, university professors, corporate executives. I felt sure that people would flock to their home, given half a chance.

"We only moved in fairly recently," said Serge, "and we find our neighbours a little ... standoffish." He selected a cigarette; in light of what he'd told me earlier, I wondered if he would smoke it inside.

"Yeah, people around here can be like that," I said. And I could see it. I could see that many of the people I knew would, like Barb, be suspicious of Serge and Selina. Many would resent their wealth and breeding. It wasn't too much of a stretch.

Serge lit his cigarette. "But you're not," he said. "You're not standoffish." He inhaled deeply, hungrily.

"I guess I just like meeting new people," I said. And I did—I really did: I just didn't often have the opportunity.

"That's a good trait, Charlie," said Serge. "Don't lose it. Never lose it. Now, I'm feeling badly that Selina and I have to slip away so soon, but I have a plan to make it up to you."

"Oh, you don't need to—" I began, but Serge cut me off.

"How would you like to come to Selina's birthday dinner on Friday?" he said.

"Yes!" I said, thrilled. "Yes, I would. Thank you!"

"You'd like that?" he smiled. "We'll begin with a good long swim, and have a real gourmet dinner afterwards. And I have some music I think you might enjoy: something different from what most of your friends are playing on their stereos, I imagine."

"I'd really like to come," I said. He had no idea how much. Or did he? Did they both see and feel my hunger?

"Good," said Serge. "That's settled, then. Now, I don't want you to worry about dressing up. Come casual. And let's have no nonsense about bringing a gift, either: you need to save for college."

While he was speaking Milly had come in. She stood waiting patiently to be noticed, her hands folded in front of her. I noticed that she kept her eyes cast down.

"Ah, here's Milly," said Serge. "She'll take you to one of the spare bedrooms so you can change."

"Okay, then," I said, rising. "Thanks. Thanks a lot. For everything, I mean."

"My pleasure, Charlie," said Serge. "See you in a few moments."

I followed Milly out of the room. As we left I glanced back and saw that I'd been sitting in front of a small abstract painting made up of black circles on a bright yellow background. My eye could make no sense of the pattern.

Is it possible that there were so few good influences in my young life? Could it really have been restricted to Mr. Boone, and now, as I saw it, Serge and Selina? The answer is no, but it's a qualified no.

I'd had other good teachers, certainly, before I entered Mr. Boone's grade twelve history course, but it was in the way of things that my contact with those people was limited to the classroom. My teachers in grade two and six were, I now recognize, pretty special people—caring, kind, and decent—but I was with them for one year each, and then I moved on. In addition, we weren't churchgoers, Barb and I, so we were cut off from the community of good folk we might well have discovered had we gone regularly to any of the six churches in Greenfield. And Barb had never been a Brownie or Girl Scout, so she wasn't interested in enrolling me in Cubs or Boy Scouts, and there was never the money to buy me the equipment I would have needed to play organized team sports in the village.

Neighbours? Again, there were some good ones, even in the relatively rundown neighbourhood I grew up in. I used to know a Mrs. Haggerty, just next door, who would give me a glass of milk and a cookie after school if Barb wasn't home, and there had been some nice people, from time to time, living in the other apartments in the house I grew up in. But we led such atomized, fragmented lives in those days. Work was usually a car ride away, and people were tired when they came home. Those who had money took their holidays elsewhere, far away from Greenfield; and those who didn't have money either didn't have holidays because they had to work all the time, or sank into a profound lethargy, rousing only to drink a few beers on their front porches on a summer's evening. Ours wasn't a vibrant culture: mostly, people watched television. Oh my God, we watched television.

I've already told you about the problems I had getting together with kids I liked from my own school. Part of it had to have been my fault. Maybe there was something about me, about my desire to be other than I was, that other kids found off-putting. Maybe a more dynamic youngster would have found ways—*created* ways—to hook up with friends. But if that's true, and I have enough self-awareness to see that it may have been, Serge and Selina's acceptance of me, their *embrace* of me, was all the more precious.

I followed Milly down a long hallway and felt that I was entering a different part of the house. There were doors on either side, and as we approached one it opened suddenly and Selina came out wearing bikini bottoms and still fiddling with the clasp of her bikini top. For just a moment, for a whisker on the face of time, I caught sight of a white breast, and my imagination instantly supplied a rosy nipple. "Holy God!" I thought, and my heart leapt into my throat.

"Aren't you coming?" asked Selina, smiling.

I stared at her. "What?" I said.

"Aren't you coming for a swim?" she said. "Hurry up and change!" And she brushed past me, and headed back down the hall, leaving me again, after a long wistful moment, to follow Milly's slight figure to the final door in the hall where, she signalled, I could enter and strip down to my swimsuit. Inside the guest bedroom I fumbled with my clothes. When I caught sight of my face in a mirror I saw that my cheeks were flushed, but I didn't need the mirror to tell me I was aroused.

THREE

I went back home to find Barb frying sausages and, unusually for her, singing along with the radio. She stopped as soon as she heard the front door close. We didn't speak for the first moment or two after I came into the kitchen, but she could not contain her curiosity for long.

"So how did things go with your fag friend?" Her voice had a harshness I hadn't fully registered before.

"He's not a fag," I said. "He has a beautiful wife."

"Boy-bait," said Barb, not in the least fazed. "What was their name again?" She took a kitchen rag and wiped grease off the counter near the burner.

"Boorman." I leaned back against the sink and watched her. Her hair was wet, and I guessed she was fresh from the shower.

"They're probably Jews," she said. "Rich Jews."

I was pretty sure they weren't, and had enough liberalism in me to find her stereotyping offensive. Mr. Boone had spent a whole period talking about anti-Semitism and the Holocaust. I said nothing, but I found that I was able to see my mother as if from a distance.

"What did they want from you?" she asked. "Other than the obvious." A Ponderosa commercial came on the radio, and she leaned over and turned it off. We'd never been to a Ponderosa. When we ate out, it was at McDonald's—and even that was a rare treat.

"They didn't want anything from me," I said. I should simply have left the room, but something in me wanted to share what I'd experienced. Even with Barb.

"They must have wanted something," said Barb, looking at me for the first time that morning.

"They gave me coffee and cake and we had a swim," I said. "And they've invited me to Selina's birthday party on Friday."

"Who's she?" asked Barb. "Their kid?"

"Selina is Mrs. Boorman," I said.

Barb thought for a moment, and pushed her sausages around the frying pan viciously. "Don't expect me to fork out money for a birthday present," she said.

"I don't expect you to do anything, Mom." It was true. I wanted to insulate my experience with them from my life with her. I wanted a firewall.

"Good," said Barb. "I'm going out. When I've had these." She turned the burner off.

"Okay," I said. Her sausages looked repulsive. I couldn't imagine Serge or Selina making a meal out of such things.

"There are a couple more in the fridge," she said, gesturing with her head.

"I'm not hungry," I said. "I'll just have a pop for now." I thought the conversation was over, and I fetched myself a root beer from the fridge and began to drink it at the kitchen sink, looking out for the mother robin. But Barb was still thinking things through.

"So they're really rich?" she said, sprinkling salt lavishly on her plate.

"I guess so," I said.

"Nice house," said Barb. It was a statement more than a question.

"Yeah," I said.

"This could be good for you. Good for both of us." She poured some ketchup on her sausages. Barb liked ketchup. When we did go to McDonald's, she grabbed handfuls of the little ketchup packages and dumped them in her purse.

"What do you mean?" I couldn't see where this was going.

"Rich people have nice things," she said. "If they offer you something, take it. Take it even if you don't have a use for it."

"Why?" I asked.

"Because *I* might," she said. "I'm serious. And if you see them putting out something for the Salvation Army or Saint V. de P.—you grab it. Offer to take it round for them. And bring it back to me."

"You want me to steal their cast-offs?" I said, incredulously.

Barb's voice grew hard and cold. "I want you to pull your goddamn weight and bring home something we can use," she said. "I'm sick of being the only breadwinner around here."

A rebellious flame flickered in me: "Collecting mother's allowance makes you a breadwinner?" I said, pushing her further than I'd ever pushed before.

Barb looked at me through narrowed eyes. "Are you sassing me, boy?" she said. "Are you sassing me? Because if you want to move out, don't think I'm stopping you. I'd be a lot more comfortable without you moping about, eating all the food in the fridge."

In the face of her anger, my flame went out. I'd never succeeded in facing down Barb—she was too strong, too overpowering. When I was younger I'd threaten to run away when we had an argument, and her response would always be enthusiastic. "Great!" she'd say—"I'll pack your things!" And she would grab a couple of plastic shopping bags and start throwing in underwear, socks, T-shirts, and a toothbrush. It was clear to me that she could envision a life without me much more clearly than I could imagine a life without her. Back then that was enough to stop me cold.

Even now, I don't fully understand where her rage came from—this sense that the world was forever cheating her out of her entitlements. I don't mean this as naively as it sounds: of course there are lots of people who feel that life owes them an easy living. What I mean is that I don't find that kind of anger in myself. When she was angry, Barb *ex*ploded. When I'm angry, I *im*plode. I lose heart. I doubt myself. At least, I used to be that way.

"I'm sorry, Mom," I said.

"You'd better be sorry," she said. "You got quite a mouth, you know that?"

"I just didn't like you attacking my friends," I said, avoiding her eyes.

"Oh, so they're your *friends* now, are they?" she said, her voice picking up mockingly on the tremor in my own. "And what would rich Jews want with a pimply-arsed little brat like you? Eh? *Friends!* I'm the one friend you've got in this world, boy, and don't you forget it."

"Okay, Mom," I said, thoroughly beaten.

"Don't you forget it," she repeated.

"Okay," I said, looking at the floor.

"All right, then," said Barb. "Now get out and let me eat my sausages in peace."

I went up to my room and lay down on my bed. I felt whipped. My world seemed smaller and darker again. But depressed though I was, I was young and could not forget the sight of Selina's white breast as she fastened her bikini top. And the memory was powerful enough that I soon got up and locked my door.

Barb went out forty minutes after I went upstairs, and hearing the front door slam was my signal that it was safe to come out. I didn't do so immediately, though; I'd begun to read *Oliver Twist* for about the eighth time. I'd been reading it obsessively for two years—finishing it, and then starting it all over again. It's funny, you know: you'd think that reading that particular book might have opened my eyes a little to what I was heading into, but book learning, I've discovered, doesn't always transfer to living in the real world. Or am I undervaluing what it taught me? Did it show me that wickedness can wear the colours of fellowship and humility?

I was deep into my book when I heard a familiar whistling

outside my bedroom window. It was Randy: he could produce, with pursed lips, a weirdly accurate copy of a chord progression in a Led Zeppelin song—I don't remember its name now. That was what our culture was about, come to think of it: television, yes, I've already said that, but also the rock we heard on AM radio. (My favourites were Rod Stewart's "Sailing" and Paul Simon's "My Little Town," but I can still remember listening open-mouthed to Donna Summer's multiple orgasms on "Love to Love You, Baby.") I waved, then went downstairs to let him in.

"How's it hangin'?" he asked, as he came into the front hall. It was a popular greeting in those days.

"Okay, I guess," I said, closing the door behind him.

"Mine's as stiff as a flagpole," he said, grabbing his crotch.

"Not right now, I hope," I said. A little joke.

"Nothin' to do with you," said Randy. "I just saw Susan Ashe in the hardware store. God, she's got a pair on her." His acne was worse than ever, but he'd traded his usual black T-shirt for one with a large RUSH logo, red on black.

"Yup, she's something," I said. "Wanna go for a walk?" It was hard knowing how to spend time with him.

"Okay," said Randy. He sniffed. "You been eating sausages?"

"Mom was," I said. "Let's get out of here." I pulled on my shoes.

We left the house, went back round the side, and set off down the street. As luck would have it, the woman from Peterborough was outside Donny's house, banging on his front door. "Come on, Donny," she shouted as we went by. "You need to get in some groceries! You need some fresh groceries, Donny! Don't think you can hide in there!"

"Is that the Christian Nazi?" asked Randy. I'd told him about her, but he'd never seen her in action.

"Yup," I said. "Isn't she a beaut?"

"What a fruitcake," he said. We passed on without further comment, taking Reid Street to Concession, then walking along Coyle until we reached the railroad tracks. They were still used, back then: a train came through once a week. We'd grown up putting pennies on the rails. We didn't talk for a couple of minutes, just stood waiting to see if the train might come along. This was roughly the right time. On the other side of the tracks we could see the fields where I often walked, the odd tree asserting itself here and there. A good number of them were elms.

"Jake was actin' pretty weird the other night," said Randy, at length.

"No kidding," I said. I picked a piece of switchgrass from beside the tracks and idly tried to peel it into strips.

"He gets into these moods," he said.

"I don't want to spend time with him, Randy," I said. The switchgrass proved resistant to peeling. I was discovering a resistance in myself, too: a growing resolve that I had no interest in a social world in which people like Jake figured at all.

"Yeah. Well." Randy shrugged. "So what've you been doin'?"

"Not much," I said, then stepped out across the tracks. Randy followed me into the fields. "I met an interesting guy here yesterday."

"Is he new?" Randy asked, tossing his hair out of his eyes. It was something he had to do quite often.

"Well, sort of," I said. "He and his wife moved here a few weeks ago."

"Oh, he's an old guy, eh?" said Randy. Anyone who was married was, of course, old.

"Forty, forty-five, maybe," I said. "Nice wife."

"How do you know?" asked Randy. He had taken out a pack of cigarettes and clearly wanted to light one, but I didn't want to stop again right that instant.

"I was over to their house for coffee," I said, trying hard to sound casual.

"Today?" asked Randy. I had surprised him.

"Yeah," I said. "They've got a nice place."

"Where do they live?" I had quickened my pace to discourage him from smoking.

"On Hazelwood," I said. "They've got a pool off to one side of the house. And a pond out back. And a really neat garden."

"Why did they invite you for coffee?" asked Randy.

"Just to be friendly—" I began, but at that moment we heard

a volley of angry barks, and we turned to see a large black dog bearing down on us at top speed. I don't know anything about dog breeds, but I do know I hadn't seen so fierce an animal before that day, and I haven't seen one since. We froze.

"Jesus!" said Randy. While he did not move, I could see that his neck, like mine, had stiffened and his jaw muscles tightened. Absurdly, weirdly, my mind conjured up a fleeting image of Milly, the Boormans' Filipino maid.

In a matter of seconds—seconds!—the dog came to within a few feet of us, then stopped. Its teeth were bared in a snarl, and it was slobbering. The word *rabies* went through my mind.

"Do you think it might bite us?" I said stupidly.

The dog barked again, then crouched as though it were going to spring. My stomach was churning, and my bowels had turned to water.

"Jesus, Jesus, Jesus," said Randy.

I've had a few of those moments in my life—moments when I was sure that injury or even death might be just a few seconds away. I've come close, too: I had a pretty serious car accident six years ago, and just recently, as I've told you, I was hit by lightning in a swimming pool. Just two days before this walk, for that matter, I'd wondered whether Jake was going to come after me with a cue. But I think this occasion was, hands-down, the one time in my life I was most scared, most physically frightened. The dog looked as if it could rip both of us apart.

And then, as quickly as the threat had appeared, it vanished. The creature seemed suddenly to hear a command from afar—a command we could not ourselves hear. It gave a final low growl, then turned and went bounding back across the field, over the railroad tracks, and into the village. In just a little more than half a minute it had passed completely out of our sight. And we were left there, shocked, shaking, fearful—conscious, suddenly and dramatically, of our smallness, our vulnerability; reminded that while teenage boys can experience moments of tremendous potency, their confidence is a thin veneer on a profound frailty. I had come within a hairsbreadth of soiling myself.

Randy swore profusely and obscenely, then lapsed into silence. I didn't want to say anything. We stood there looking back to where the dog had disappeared, both of us wondering whether we dared return by that same route. Where had the animal come from? Why wasn't it leashed?

"It must belong to visitors," I said at last, wanting to reassure myself as much as anything else. But it was certainly strange neither of us had seen the creature before.

"I nearly shit myself," said Randy, and that made me feel a little better. He lit a cigarette, and wordlessly offered me the pack, even knowing I didn't smoke. I wanted one, wanted the infusion of courage I suspected it might give me, but I shook my head no. We moved on.

"I'm going there on Friday for her birthday party," I said.

"What? Going where?" said Randy, his focus understandably elsewhere.

"To the Boormans. The house of the guy I met in the fields," I said. My fear was receding quickly. My friendship with the Boormans, so new and fresh, was fast becoming the dominant reality in my life.

"So whose birthday party are we talking about?"

"Selina's. His wife's. We're swimming and having a big dinner and everything."

Randy was silent for a moment. Then, turning to me: "Why would you want to go to some old broad's birthday?"

"She's not old," I said. "She's just turning thirty-two, and she's beautiful."

"Women are getting old at thirty-two," said Randy. "Their tits sag, and they get fat." He farted loudly, as if to lend force to his judgment.

"Not Selina," I said, remembering vividly how she'd looked in her bikini. "She's amazing."

"A real babe, eh?" said Randy. His focus was returning.

"She's beautiful," I confirmed. We resumed our walk. It was another sunny day, for the moment, though I could see dark clouds to the north. Randy sucked on his cigarette. Most of the people I knew in Greenfield in those days were serious smokers. There was a large student smoking area behind the high school, and whenever you knocked on the staff room door and someone opened you were practically knocked over by the smell.

"Do you think you can get a piece?" he said, suddenly.

"What?"

"Do you figure you can get some? You know what I mean. If she looks a real babe and her old man's that much older, she's probably hot for it."

"I don't think so," I said. But the thought was intriguing.

"You gonna try, even?" said Randy, his face again twisted up as he turned towards me.

"She's *married*," I said.

"So?" said Randy. "Married broads screw around all the time."

"Serge is a nice guy," I said weakly.

"Then he won't mind sharing," said Randy. "Do you think she'd like to have a couple of young bucks at the same time? Or, hey, Charlie, just introduce me and step aside. I know what a woman needs." This struck me as ridiculous, but his conviction was so strong I did not laugh at him. Still, I hated the thought of him being with Selina. If anyone aside from Serge were going to enjoy her, it would have to be me. But I knew I hadn't the nerve even to try.

I've told you some harsh things about Barb, and the picture gets even grimmer, but she was maybe a little more complex than I've suggested. My grandmother Edna—Barb's mother—lived in Peterborough, and all the years Edna was alive, Barb would hitch a ride with someone every couple of weeks and pay her a visit. Edna was a large, fleshy woman, and she smelled of sweat, and something else. Urine, maybe.

On one occasion, when I was about twelve, Barb took me along with her. She used her own key to open the door, and we came in to find Edna watching *The Price is Right* on television, the sound turned up very loud, a glass of gin and a bottle of Tums at her elbow.

"Hello, Mom," said Barb.

"Hi," said Edna, not taking her eyes off the television. A fat woman in a muumuu was trying to guess the price of a home spa.

"I've brought you some groceries," Barb said. She was carrying a plastic bag filled with canned soups, condensed milk, bread, and baked beans.

"Okay," my grandmother answered. She had a deep voice for a woman. Her floral print dress was soiled. Her toenails were so long they were beginning to curl. I catalogued her imperfections.

Barb looked at Edna a moment, then headed towards the kitchen. I sat down in the living room, but my grandmother just ignored me. I couldn't compete with Bob Barker and Dian Parkinson.

So while Edna sat watching television, and I sat watching Edna, Barb cleaned up her kitchen. She wasn't a great housekeeper herself, but she washed the many days' worth of dishes she found in the sink and on the counters, and she collected the empty gin bottles and tucked them away in an empty cardboard box. She unpacked the groceries she'd bought, and arranged them in the poorly stocked cupboards. When she'd done all that, she made her mother a sandwich.

Edna, meanwhile, took a sip of gin, swallowed it, opened the bottle of Tums, took a couple, and popped them into her mouth. Her eyes never left the television. I watched her with horrified fascination. Remarkably, her right hand did not shake at all, but she used her left as little as possible.

Barb came into the room with the sandwich on a plate. "Here we are, Mom," she said. "I made you a cheese and ketchup sandwich."

"Okay," said Edna.

Barb put the plate down beside her mother, and stood looking at her for a moment. At last aware of being scrutinized, Edna looked at her briefly, without emotion, then turned her eyes back to the television.

Barb gestured to me to come. "See you later, Mom," she said to Edna. Edna said nothing—simply took a swig of gin. We left. Barb didn't say a word while we waited for our ride home.

Four

On the Friday of that week I returned to the Boormans' house, ringing the doorbell with a great deal more confidence than I had the last. I stood straddling the welcome mat, clutching my rolled towel in one hand and a small wrapped gift in the other, swinging both arms. Milly opened the door.

"Good afternoon, Mr. Charlie," she said.

"Hi, Milly," I replied. "Am I too early?"

"No, you are right when you were expected," she said, still very formal, still avoiding contractions. "Please come in." She stepped aside.

I stepped inside. "Where are Serge and Selina?"

"They are by the pool," she said. "I will take you to the guest bedroom so you can change." She was wearing the same modest blue dress, and her pale skin was still untouched by makeup.

"Thanks," I said, and I again followed her. Milly moved very gracefully, but her gait was more womanly than girlish, it seemed to me: it was something in the swing of her hips. The house was large enough that I still wasn't certain where to turn left, where to turn right. "How old are you, Milly?" I asked. The question surprised even me with its out-of-the-blue gaucheness.

If Milly was surprised, she didn't show it. "I am twenty-two," she said quietly. She didn't stop.

"Have you always been a maid?" I was just a step or two behind her.

"No," said Milly. "Once I was a student like you, but my family was large and I needed to work to help support them."

"Was this in Canada?"

"The Philippines," she said. We had arrived at the doorway to one of the guest bedrooms.

"Did you become a maid right away?" I pressed her.

"I worked as a seamstress in Lebanon," she replied, "then I was offered a post in Egypt looking after children. From Egypt I came to Canada to work for another family. Then I got sick." Her lower lip may have trembled just for a moment.

"What were you sick with?" I asked. This time she hesitated before answering. It was the briefest of hesitations, but it told me she was uncomfortable. Still, I said nothing to take the question back.

"I had a nervous breakdown," she said. "It is hard coming from another country and not knowing anyone." She looked me in the eyes. "Is there anything else you need?"

"No. No, thank you," I said—and I'd like to think I had the grace to blush.

"Can you find your way to the pool from here?" Milly asked. While Selina smelled of exotic perfume, Milly smelled simply of soap. Ordinary bar soap.

"Yeah, I think so," I said. "It's to the side of the house, isn't it? Over there," I gestured broadly. "Are you eating dinner with us?" I asked as she turned to go.

She turned back and looked at me again. "I am serving dinner," she said.

This hadn't occurred to me—though it should have. "Don't you ever get time off?" I asked.

She smiled wanly, then turned away again. "No," she said. And she left.

"Oh," I said to her retreating back. And that didn't seem fair. I felt a surge of sympathy for her, but it didn't last long.

I peeled off my shorts and my T-shirt, folded them (after a fashion), and put them on the double bed in the guest bedroom. It was a very nice room, decorated, if I remember correctly, in pastel greens and blues. There was a full-length mirror on one of the walls, and I went over to it and examined myself critically. I was not, I saw, a particularly handsome young man, but, like Barb, I'd somehow managed to avoid putting on excess pounds, and my legs, at least, were reasonably muscular. I had then, as I have still, broad shoulders, and my hair, on this day at any rate, was clean and well brushed. "Passable," I said to the image in the mirror. "Passable." After a moment's thought I dropped my swimsuit and saw my privates as another person might. "Bigger than average," I decided hopefully. I was thinking of Selina, however, and that inevitably had a distorting effect, so I pulled my swimsuit up again, and did a little jog on the spot in the hope that the exercise would make me presentable at poolside.

Back through the house I went, this time, however, avoiding the living room (which would have taken me to the back garden), and going straight somewhere instead. I stepped out the side door and into the pool enclosure that I'd already visited once before. Serge and Selina were stretched out in two of four long deck chairs: Selina was in a small white bikini, and Serge in a boxer-style swimsuit. I was carrying my wrapped gift (a bar of *luxury soap* purchased from the drugstore) in one hand, and my now-unrolled towel in the other.

"Here's the bright young knight!" said Serge, waving cheerily. He looked tanned and handsome.

"Our shining prince!" cried Selina, smiling a warm welcome. No one had ever called me a *knight* and a *prince* before. One of Barb's ex-boyfriends had given me what I'd thought was an affectionate nickname, "SF," but Barb told me, after he'd dumped her, that it stood for "Shit-Face."

"Hi," I said, smiling goofily, and I went over to them. "Happy birthday, Selina," I added, and I offered her my gift. A lady in the drugstore had wrapped it for me.

"Oh, you shouldn't have spent money on me!" said Selina, beaming fit to break my heart. She took it from my hands.

"He's a bad boy, Selina," said Serge. "I told him not to trouble himself."

"It was very wrong of you," said Selina. "But very sweet, too." She laughingly shook the gift, as if this would tell her what it was.

"It's nothing big," I said. "Just a small thing, really." Of course I didn't tell them that I'd stolen the money from Barb's purse to buy it. I didn't feel good about that: I felt it diminished me. But it would have shamed me to show up without a present.

Selina unwrapped the package slowly, exclaiming over how nicely it was wrapped. When she revealed the bar of soap she held it to her nose and breathed in deeply. "Oh, Serge," she said, "it's a bar of my favourite soap. Mmm, smell that, darling. Charlie, that was too generous of you." She held her arms wide and signalled that she wanted a kiss. I bent down and presented my cheek, but she put her hand gently on my face and brought my lips to hers. She tasted like coconut milk and honey.

"Do you really like it?" I asked. My pulse was racing.

"I love it," said Selina. "I'll use it in my shower after our swim."

Serge laughed. "And she'll insist that you smell her, Charlie, and drive me mad with jealousy!"

I had no idea then what Serge might mean, and my face must have betrayed my bewilderment. "Oh, don't tease our friend, Serge," said Selina, giving him a dismissive wave. "Charlie, the water is the perfect temperature. You must dive straight in and show us what you can do."

"Okay," I said, happy to have a diversion. "Should I go in off the board?" I wasn't a bad diver, having learned how at the quarry about a quarter mile from town. The quarry had been drained a couple of summers before in response to a drowning, but I'd practised for hours on end before the site was closed.

"Yes, off the board," said Selina. "Go on. We'll watch you."

"Watch this, then!" I said. "I can do a jackknife!" I stepped up, felt the give under my feet, and ran at the water, bouncing at the end of the board. It wasn't a perfect dive, but it wasn't a bad one either.

Have you ever taken your kids to the swimming pool? *Mommy, watch this! Daddy, watch me.* Watch *me!* I'd never been watched before. When I reached the surface of the water I looked eagerly to Serge and Selina for approval ... and they were both watching. They both applauded. I was in heaven.

"Bravo, bravo!" said Selina, laughing happily and continuing to clap.

"You must teach me how, Charlie," cried Serge.

I was in heaven.

About eight months before that summer, in November of 1974, I had asked Barb if she would mind looking at an assignment I had written for my English class. It was a response to a poem, Wordsworth's "The World Is Too Much With Us." My teacher had told us to read it carefully, then write a poem of our own that expressed some of the same thoughts and feelings. I don't know, maybe it wasn't a brilliant assignment, but I didn't mind doing it. Anyway, Barb read the first part of Wordsworth's poem, but got sidetracked by the line that reads, "This Sea that bares her bosom to the moon."

"What's that supposed to mean?" she asked.

"I think it means that the Sea shows its nakedness," I said. "I mean, there it is, and it doesn't try to hide what it is. And it's beautiful. I think that's what it means." I liked the poem: it stirred something in me that wasn't often stirred. I liked the way the words felt in my mouth.

Barb had been drinking. "I don't want to look at this shit," she said. "You tell that idiot teacher of yours that I don't want you reading this sort of crap."

"What do you want me to read?" I asked, feeling, on this occasion as on so many others, stirrings of abortive defiance.

"Job postings," she said succinctly. And that was that.

After we'd swum, Serge directed me to a full bathroom near the guest bedroom, and I showered there while he and Selina showered in their ensuite bathroom and dressed for dinner. Selina said they'd be half an hour, and invited me to make myself at home if I finished sooner than that. I made my way to the living room, and stood for several minutes staring out the French doors at the garden. The sun had not yet gone down, but the shadows were lengthening and nocturnal creatures beginning, I imagined, to open their eyes and ready themselves for foraging. It was not quite dusk, though, and I was not altogether surprised to see two hawks high overhead. Beautiful birds, I thought: beautiful and dangerous.

Milly appeared quietly and, seeing me standing there, offered me a drink.

I asked: "What is there?"

"There are many soft drinks," she said, "and there is wine, too." If she realized how astonishing this offer was, nothing on her face revealed it.

"Do you think I *could* have wine?" I asked, amazed at the thought.

"Mrs. Boorman said you may have anything you like," said Milly. So I asked for wine, and I was brought a glass of a glowing red a couple of minutes later. I sat and sipped it sitting in one of the plush armchairs I'd marvelled at before. Truth be told, I didn't much like the taste of it, but I liked the way it warmed my throat. As I sat there, staring into the living room, my back once again to the black and yellow abstract painting, I thought, *this is the kind of life I want: a life with a spacious home, and a beautiful garden, and a swimming pool, and a servant, and a lovely wife.* And I wondered what I could do, what on earth I could do, to engineer a future very different from the one for which I seemed headed as a small-town boy from the House of Barb.

Serge came before Selina: he'd changed into an elegant green kimono—though I had no idea what it was when he first appeared. "I'm fascinated by Japanese culture," he said casually. We sat chatting for a few moments, and then Selina joined us, looking radiant in a sleek black dress with ruby earrings. It's funny that I remember that detail all these years later, but I found myself transfixed by them at times during dinner. They seemed to contain their own inner fire.

And what an extraordinary dinner it was. We sat at a long oak table in a dining room with high ceilings and two points of entry—one from the kitchen where Milly was cooking and from which she served. There was a floral centrepiece on the table, and it was flanked by silver candlesticks. The cutlery was silver, too, while the crockery was hand-painted bone china. I know that because at one point I noticed that the designs were not precisely uniform, and Serge explained, casually, that they'd sat and watched while a Korean artist wielded the brush. Milly had lit the candles before we came in, but she'd also left the crystal chandelier above the table on at a subdued setting. She served us a vichyssoise to begin, then swordfish steaks with baby potatoes and carrots and snap peas. After she had cleared the main course, we tucked into a dessert of ice cream with raspberries served in chocolate sauce. Classical music was playing quietly from speakers set into a side table. I couldn't believe what I was eating. I couldn't believe I was there.

"Milly is going to bring us our liqueurs in the living room," said Serge. "What will you have, Charlie?"

"I don't know," I said. "I've never had a liqueur. I mean, I've heard of them, but I've never actually tasted one." A second glass of wine had left me formidably relaxed and ready for just about anything.

"Will you let me choose for you?" asked Serge. He looked very assured and comfortable in his kimono. I began to wish that I had one, too.

"Yes, please," I said.

"Are we all finished, then?" said Serge. "Yes? Take Charlie in, Selina. I'll be with you in a moment."

Serge got up and left the room. Selina put her serviette on the table, smiled at me, rose, and slipped her arm through mine as we headed towards the living room. I'd not previously realized that moving from one room to another could be in any sense an event, but it clearly was. I drank in the smell of Selina's perfume—a muskier scent than the one she'd worn earlier in the evening. She walked in such a way that I could feel her right breast against my arm.

"This is the nicest birthday party I can remember," she said. "I have two handsome men all to myself."

"It's the nicest birthday I can remember, too," I said. We went into the living room together, the passages and entries wide enough to permit us to remain arm in arm. Milly had clearly come in while we were eating and lit candles. There was also a pleasantly pungent smell in the air.

"It's incense, Charlie," said Selina. She drew my attention to a small incense burner on the mantelpiece. "We have a friend in India who sends us a package every year." She sat down on a sofa, slipped off her shoes, and tucked her legs up underneath her. "What do you do on your birthdays?" she asked.

"Mom usually gets a cake from the IGA, and we have hot dogs or something," I said. The thought that I'd ever found this exciting embarrassed me suddenly. My life, I saw, was unspeakably banal.

"That must be nice," said Selina, smiling still. "Just you and your mom?"

"Sometimes her boyfriend is there," I said. "It depends who she's seeing."

"And do you like her present boyfriend?" Selina looked thoughtful and grave suddenly.

"He's not the worst she's had," I said. I wanted to change the subject. "Selina, why did you and Serge come here when you could have gone anywhere?"

Selina massaged one of her calves with her hand. Like Serge, she thought about her answers before giving them. "It's quiet," she said, after a moment. "And the countryside is lovely. We both love trees and gardens and lakes."

"Yeah, but the people are so ... boring," I said. "You know what they do for fun? They get drunk and they watch television and sometimes they go to hockey games. And that's it. There isn't even a movie theatre in town."

"Well, that makes finding a good friend or two particularly important," said Selina. "I'm so glad Serge met you in the fields, Charlie."

"I am, too," I said fervently. "Believe me." The wine had left me feeling mellow and sentimental. To my astonishment, the intensity of my emotion—my gratitude, my sense of being blessed—brought tears to my eyes. It did not seem a manly thing, and I hoped desperately that Selina would not notice.

At that moment, Serge entered, carrying a tray with three liqueur glasses. They were filled with a green liquid that twinkled in the candlelight. It occurred to me that it matched the colour of his outfit.

"Chartreuse for three," said Serge. "I've told Milly to finish the dishes and go to bed," he added quietly, to Selina.

"Thank you, Serge," said Selina, taking the glass he offered her. "Charlie, you're in for a treat."

"It's green," I said, looking at the glass she held in her hand.

"It's green, and it tastes of emeralds," said Selina. "It's heavenly. Sip it."

"Play with it on your tongue," said Serge, bowing as he handed me my glass.

I sipped, and found it good. Very good. Sweeter than the wine, and my palate liked sweetness.

"I want to propose a toast," said Serge, raising his glass and looking at Selina. "To the woman who, nearly twelve years ago, made me the happiest man on earth when she accepted my invitation to wed. To the woman who grows more beautiful with each passing year. To the woman whose kindness makes her seem, at times, an angel in mortal guise. Happy birthday, darling."

I raised my own glass. "Happy birthday, Selina," I said enthusiastically. (How I wished *I* could call her *darling*.)

"Oh, Serge. You're so good to me," said Selina. And she slipped off the sofa and slipped into his arms, pulling him to her and meeting his lips with hers.

Serge kissed her warmly, but it was he who broke off the kiss. "But you haven't had your birthday present yet," he said.

"I've had my soap!" Selina said, smiling at me.

"Yes," said Serge, "and it's wonderful soap. But you haven't had your present from me!"

Selina seemed also childlike in her excitement: "What is it! What is it?" she cried. Just an ounce less restraint would have seen her jumping up and down.

"Can you guess?" asked Serge, beaming at her. He was, in that moment, as I imagined a loving and indulgent father might be.

"No, no!" cried Selina. "Give it to me, Serge!" And she did jump, just once, clasping her hands together and laughing.

"Can *you* guess, Charlie?" asked Serge, turning to me.

I was completely caught up in Selina's excitement, and found myself laughing also. "No, I don't know either," I said. "Let's see it!"

Serge looked from one of us to the other, prolonging the anticipation as long as he reasonably could. Then he turned towards the hallway. "Milly!" he called.

Milly entered. She must have been standing in the hallway, just out of our sight. She had put on high-heeled shoes, black stockings, and a slinky yellow dress with a sash at the back. She'd also applied makeup, I saw, but had applied it thickly and inexpertly enough that it made her look younger rather than older. As she came towards us, she tried to move like a fashion model on a runway.

Selina clapped her hands: "Milly!" she cried. "Is Milly my present?"

"No, no!" said Serge laughing. "Though she'd make a lovely present, wouldn't she? No, Milly is simply the charming vehicle."

"What is it, Serge?" said Selina. "I can't bear waiting!"

Serge beckoned Milly to go to him, and she went. She stood next to him, on his left, looking into his face, and then, at the smallest of gestures from him, she looked at us. Her face was expressionless, but the combination of her makeup, her dress, her shoes, and her posture made me ache sexually. I was suddenly conscious that she too was a desirable creature—not on the same level as Selina, perhaps, but more than ripe enough for me to despoil a thousand times in my imaginary debauches.

"Watch the magician," said Serge, and his right hand strayed to Milly's belly. He lingered there briefly, caressing it for a moment, then twisted his wrist and turned his hand out, fingers splayed, to show that it was empty. He then put his right index finger back on her belly, and traced an imaginary line from her belly button round her hip to the small of her back, walking around her as he moved his finger. He paused, and looked at us.

"Show me! Show me!" cried Selina, her lips parted just a little.

Serge withdrew his hand from behind Milly's back, from the folds of the sash, to show that he was holding a decorated golden egg.

"It's a solid gold egg," he said quietly, "covered in rubies and sapphires."

"No!" breathed Selina—she was almost speechless with delight.

"Yes," said Serge. "How else to honour beauty but with beauty?" He had come round to Milly's side again, and was facing us fully. His left hand, however, had moved behind her waist, and it seemed to me, just for a second or two, that he must be massaging her back, or perhaps a little lower.

And that was the moment when I first realized that something was not quite right. What it was, I couldn't have articulated then, but something in me, something at the centre of my admittedly underdeveloped moral sense, *twitched*. It was as though I had been sitting in a concert hall listening to a marvellous symphony orchestra, and suddenly the first violinist broke a string. The recognition didn't last long—I soon shoved it aside—but it was there nonetheless.

Selina went to Serge and kissed him passionately. (Milly averted her eyes, but I could not tear mine away.) Selina then fell to a close examination of the egg, moving her fingers across the jewels as if she were reading a particularly intricate passage in Braille.

"You can go now, Milly," said Serge, a little curtly. And she left, headed, perhaps, back to the kitchen. I watched her go—watched the small twitch of the sash, the silkiness of the stockings, the calculated vulnerability of the high heels.

"It's absolutely breathtaking, Serge," said Selina. She kissed the egg.

"Is it really solid gold?" I asked. The idea seemed stunning.

"Yes, it is," said Serge. "Right the way through."

"It must have cost ... *thousands*," I said. I could scarcely begin to imagine that scale of generosity. It seemed at once preposterous and wildly romantic.

"If I had them," said Serge, "I wouldn't hesitate to spend *trillions*.

You know that, don't you, my darling?" he said, putting an arm around Selina.

Selina looked at him adoringly. "I know that, Serge," she said. She touched a finger to her lips and transferred a kiss to his.

"What will you do with it?" I asked, at once revelling in the openness of their affection and feeling a sharp jealousy.

Serge laughed. "That's a very good question," he said. "What will you do with it, Selina?"

Selina was staring at it still. "Look at it, and touch it, and play with it. I'll take it out and play with it every day of my life," she said. "Would you like to see it, Charlie?"

"Sure," I said. I took it gingerly, thrilling for an instant at her fleeting touch. The egg was surprisingly heavy.

"It's all right," Selina said, a fond amusement colouring her voice. "You won't crack it."

"Yeah, I know," I said. "But I wouldn't want to, you know, knock off a ruby, or something."

"No need to worry, Charlie," said Serge. "But we appreciate your care. So many other young men would be rough with beautiful things. You have all the right instincts."

"He's so sweet," said Selina. "We're going to have to find him a nice girlfriend, Serge."

"What a wonderful project!" said Serge. They both looked at me. There was affection in their gaze, but I still felt a little embarrassed.

"Oh, I—I'm okay, there," I said. "I know lots of girls." In that instant, however, the girls I knew seemed remarkably drab—dowdy and shopworn and dull.

"I'll bet you do, Charlie," said Serge. "I'll bet you have your pick of the crop."

"If I were a teenager, I'd certainly be chasing you!" said Selina. She reached out her hand and stroked my cheek with her fingers. I wanted the moment to last forever. I wanted...

"Well, no," I said, "it's not that I can have *anyone* exactly. It's more that, you know..."

They knew, certainly, that I was confused and embarrassed,

and Serge moved swiftly to make things easy for me. "Music," he said. "We need some dance music. What would you like to hear, Selina?"

"Oh, let me think," she said. "How about, how about ... some Strauss?"

"Strauss it is," said Serge. "Be back in just a moment."

Serge slipped away, his kimono rustling slightly. I handed Selina back her egg. "It's an amazing thing," I said.

"Serge always gives amazing gifts," she said. "They're always so special. And I swear he tops himself every time." She carried the egg over to a coffee table and placed it on a little square of white cloth, then brought one of the candles nearer so that the gems could catch its fire. She stood there gazing down at her gift, and I stood six or seven feet away, devouring her with my eyes. With her focus elsewhere, and Serge out of the room, I could stare at her without fear of reproach. Her skin, her hair, the pout of her lips, the thrust of her breasts—she was a sumptuous meal to a starving man. If I'd been a dog, I would have drooled. The speakers in the room came to life suddenly, and we heard the opening bars of a Strauss waltz. Serge came back in, and went over to her.

"Madam," he said, bowing. "May I have the pleasure?"

"You may, sir," said Selina, and he took her left hand in his, and slid his right arm round her waist. As the music grew louder, they began to waltz elegantly and romantically around the room, and as for me ... I watched every move they made. I had extinguished the flicker of concern I'd felt earlier, and was simply intoxicated by their style, their grace, their elegance. They seemed to me to be everything I was not. They seemed to be like visitors from some fabulously advanced civilization light years away. Mind you, I was more conflicted, more confused, than I'd ever been before. I simultaneously worshipped Serge, and wished him back on his home planet, leaving Selina behind with me. I simultaneously adored Selina—would have fought dragons for her, brought her moon jewels, kissed her slippered feet—and wanted to strip her naked, spread her legs, and wantonly thrust myself into her. She thought me sweet? No. Not sweet. I wanted to make her cry out in passion.

"Your turn, Charlie," said Serge. The music had ended. They both stood in front of me, smiling. Selina was offering me her hand.

"I can't," I said, in a sudden state of panic.

"You can't?" said Serge, puzzled.

"I mean, I can't dance," I said. "I don't know how to, how to do that dance you were doing." (I did not then know the word *waltz*.)

"There's an easy remedy to that," said Serge, and he turned and left the room. I looked at Selina, my eyes signalling my fear.

"I will teach you, Charlie," she said, smiling. Forever smiling! Always smiling!

"What, *now*?" I said.

"Not now," she said. "Some other evening. The summer stretches out in front of us like some languorous cat. There's plenty of time."

The Strauss music had stopped, and after a moment's pause something else came on: slow-dance music. Passion pit stuff. Soft and sexy.

"Can you dance to this?" Selina asked.

"It's just ... it's just slow-dance music, isn't it?" I said. "I mean, you don't really dance, you just sort of ... move." I can do that, I thought.

"That's right," said Selina. "Come here." She held her arms open for me, and I stepped into them as one steps into a dream. It's a slipping sensation, isn't it? We don't fight the entry, no matter how hard we may later fight to leave, to wake up. We walk in, and it wraps itself around us, and the menace and the threats and the terror come later. Not that it was that kind of dream that I was entering. It was more complicated than that. And I know, I *know* that I was at once the dreamer and the dream-maker—the pony and the rider. I know the measure of my own guilt, my culpability. In any event, I slipped into her arms and, after a moment, we began to move, to turn very slowly.

"This is nice," said Selina.

I was still feeling awkward, but after a little bit I began to relax somewhat. One overpowering reality settled in: I was holding Selina in my arms. My hand was at her waist. Her face was inches from mine. "I'm getting the hang of it now," I said.

"Mmm," said Selina. Her sweet scent filled my nostrils.

"I've never actually done this," I said. "But I've seen people do it."

"Mmm," she said, and she brought her face towards me ... then rested her head on my shoulder.

"It's not hard," I said.

"Mmm," she said. Her eyes were closed.

"It's nice," I said.

"Shh-shh-shh," she said gently. "Just relax and move with the music."

I tried. I wanted to. But I was not utterly in control of my body, and Selina's scent and touch were beginning to overpower my anxiety. The dance was not hard, but something else was. I needed to talk. I needed to distract myself and, I hoped, her.

"What's ... what's Serge doing?" I asked.

"He's probably just saying good-night to Milly," said Selina. If she was aware of my changed state, she did not say anything, or alter her own behaviour in the slightest. She stayed in my arms. She continued to move with the music. Her eyes remained closed.

"Oh. Okay," I said, and I began, at last, to relax fully—to accept that this wonderful experience was happening to me. I brought Selina a little closer. I brushed her hair with my lips. I closed my own eyes. And then, just at the moment that I was about to let go the last of my fears and inhibitions—there was a loud banging on the front door of the Boorman home.

"What's that?" I said, pulling back a little, though keeping Selina in my arms.

"I don't know," said Selina, her eyes opening into cat-like slits. "But Serge will look after it, Charlie. Just keep dancing."

But the mood was lost, and just a moment later we heard the front door open and then slam shut, and Barb's loud, brazen, drunken voice approached us as its owner barrelled through the halls.

"I just want to see my little boy ... my little Charlie," said Barb. We could not yet see her. Selina gently disengaged.

"I assure you he is safe," came Serge's voice—but at that instant Barb erupted into the living room.

"There you are, Charlie," she said triumphantly. She stood staring at me and Selina, swaying ever so slightly. Her eyes were bloodshot, and she was wearing one of Roger's T-shirts with MOLSON'S emblazoned across the front.

"What are you doing, Mom?" I asked, outrage beginning its climb from my stomach to my lips.

"What am I doing?" she said indignantly. "I'm checking up on you. I'm making sure you're not being ... eaten alive by rich Jews, or something. I'm making sure you're safe."

"Of course I'm *safe*," I said. "I'm with *friends*."

"It's a pleasure to meet you, Mrs. Knowles," said Serge. He offered Barb his hand.

"Welcome to our home," said Selina, taking a step towards Barb.

"Right," said Barb. "This is one helluva place," she added, swaying a little more dangerously.

"Thank you," said Selina.

"One helluva place," repeated Barb. She zeroed in on Selina suddenly. "What do you want with my son, anyway?" she said. "It's too late to circumcise him."

"Mom!" I yelped, desperately, hopelessly embarrassed. I was confounded by Barb's weird insistence that the Boormans were Jewish, but I was even more thrown by her alluding to my genitals. It seemed to reduce me to the status of child.

"We've no interest in circumcising your son, Mrs. Knowles," said Serge smoothly. "And as it happens, we're not Jewish. But we do like books and music and gardening, and we see some of the same tastes in your son. We are honoured by his friendship. He is a great credit to you."

"His being here has made this a very special birthday party for me," said Selina. She reached out and tousled my hair, in the way a mother other than Barb might.

Barb snorted. "Him being here has made your birthday *special*," she said. "Don't make me laugh."

"I'm taking you home, Mom," I said, moving towards her.

"'Cause if I start laughing," said Barb, "I'm gonna puke." And just for a moment, I thought that she might.

"I'm warning you, Mom—" I said, very angry myself now.

"And I wouldn't want to puke cheap booze on this very expensive deep pile rug," said Barb. "You didn't get this at K-Mart, did you?" She kicked at the carpet with her foot, deliberately creating a blemish on its smooth surface.

"We're leaving," I said. I turned to Selina: "I'm so sorry—" I began.

"What's the game, eh?" said Barb. "What's the fucking game?"

In that instant, I loathed and detested her. I could not believe she was saying these poisonous, hateful things to my friends. The fact that Serge answered mildly, gently, made me feel no better. "There is no game, Mrs. Knowles," he said. "No game at all."

"Why are you wearing a dress?" demanded Barb.

"This is a kimono," said Serge, still looking at her without malice.

"What are you wearing a *fag* thing like that for?" asked my mother. I wanted the earth to swallow me up.

"Mrs. Knowles," said Selina gently: "I think you've had too much to drink."

"Let's go," I said, advancing on Barb. I took her by the elbow. "Come on. We're going."

"Don't mandle-handle—don't you manhandle me!" said Barb. "What do you think you're doing? Get your cotton-pickin' hands off me."

She slapped at me, and then tried to shove me away. Under normal circumstances that would have been enough to send me running, but these weren't normal circumstances. I grabbed her, and began wrestling her towards the door. "Come on!" I shouted. "I want you out of here!" I pushed her out of the living room, and we started down the hall, her resistance diminishing. The combination of too much booze and my unprecedented fury was, I think, taking its toll.

Behind me, I heard Selina's voice: "Don't worry, Charlie!" she called. And behind her I heard Serge: "Come back and see us!" As we moved through the front hallway I grabbed my mother with my right arm, and opened the front door with my left. We both tumbled out into the night.

FIVE

Many years after the events of that evening, I got a telephone call very late Saturday night from a good friend. Darris was a part-time art teacher at the local community college. His wife, Theresa, was a part-time school librarian. They had a beautiful five-year-old daughter, Julie, and they lived together, the three of them, in a quiet, lower-middle-class neighbourhood in Belleville. Earlier that day, Theresa had taken Julie on a trip out of town to see a pottery show and visit some friends. While they were gone, Darris had gone to a toy store and found a magic wand—a foot-long piece of plastic filled with lots of tiny stars and crescent moons floating in a blue liquid. There was a label on the wand that said that if you put it under the light for a while, it would soon glow in the dark. Darris was a sentimental fellow, and he loved his daughter with a love that knew no bounds. He bought the wand, took it home, put it on Julie's bed, and waited for his wife and child to come back.

The little girl was killed on the way home, killed in an accident. A van crossed the median and slammed into the side of the car. Late that night, after Darris had identified his daughter and been ordered from his wife's bedside at the hospital, he called me. We sat and drank whiskey together, but after a couple of hours he insisted we go into Julie's room. It was dark, pitch black ... but the wand was shining. Darris got down on his knees and howled. "I want my child—my magic, shining, singing daughter!" he cried. "I want my baby! Dear God, dear God, I want to hold her in my arms once more."

I can only imagine what a spectacle Barb and I made of ourselves as we progressed through Greenfield. She was a pace or two ahead of me and moving fast, but the booze she'd consumed made her stumble every now and then, and I was in no frame of mind to tell her to slow down and take more care. Part of me wanted her to trip and break her neck. That walk will forever be etched in my memory: Barb just one beer away from falling-down drunk but fuelled also by something I didn't (and don't) understand; and me, mostly sober, yes, but charged up with hormones, righteous indignation, corrosive embarrassment, and adolescent fury.

When we got home, she burst through the front door and I followed her into the kitchen. There, she wheeled on me.

"Leave me alone!" she shouted. She stank of alcohol—alcohol and her cheap perfume.

"Why did you do that?" I shouted back.

"Get away from me," she said, and she turned as if to go upstairs to her bedroom.

I seized her by the shoulders and spun her around. "I want to know why you're trying to wreck my life," I said, looking her full in the face.

"I'm not trying to wreck your life, you screwy pinhead," she said. "I'm trying to save you from being fucked over by two sickies!" She sprayed me with spittle.

"My friends are not sickies." I said it slowly, carefully, as though I were speaking to some particularly obtuse child.

"They're as sick as rabid monkeys, you blind asshole," said Barb—and she pulled out of my grip and went over to the sink to get herself a glass of water.

I was reduced to an impotent fury. "They are not!" I cried. "You're the sick one! You're the drunken cow! You're the one who's fucking up my life! They're the first nice thing that's ever happened to me, and you've just ruined it. You ruined it!"

"That's no way to speak to your goddamn mother!" said Barb, rounding on me again.

"I wish you weren't my goddamn mother!" I shouted.

There was a pause. I was angry, very angry, but even so I wondered if I'd gone too far. I'd never said anything remotely approaching that before.

"Oh. Oh," said Barb. "Well, then." But she was no actress, and her transparent attempt to look hurt galvanized me into going even farther.

"Don't think I'm going to fall for this act," I said. "You can't play the poor, hurt mother because you've never been a *real* mother to me. The only reason I'm alive is you left it too late to have me vacuumed out of you."

Barb's eyes narrowed. "I want you out of the house!" she hissed at me.

"If I leave," I said, "you lose your mother's allowance. You need me more than I need you."

Did that hurt? It did. Barb looked stung. But in truth, it hurt me more than it hurt her, because her expression told me that I might just be right. So that night, when I went up to my bedroom, I had a great deal to think about. I felt that my world was shifting, and that things could never be quite the same. And it seemed to me that the book of my childhood had definitively closed, and that I was opening a very different volume.

It's strange what comes back when you begin remembering a period in your life that's long past. In the year I was seventeen there was a retarded woman in Greenfield who walked up and down the streets of the village, pushing a pram. She looked very happy, very proud, but whenever she saw a boy or a man on her side of the street she made a point of crossing to the other side. There was no baby in the pram—just a doll—and on the hot summer nights of that July and August she would sit on the front porch of the rooming house where she lived and hold her doll to her breast, stroking the plastic hair, suckling the plastic lips. While I never joined the other boys in making public mock of her, I too thought her pathetic.

It's useless to moralize, but there's a part of me, however small, that worries there's a ledger kept somewhere—that my instances of arrogance and conceit, of vanity and greed, have been noted, every one, and that the small acts of kindness, all too small, all too few, will not be enough, will not be enough, will not, finally, be enough.

The next morning I made my way back to the Boormans' home, dragging my feet a little, but recognizing that I had an apology to make. My own birthdays had never been particularly special affairs, though Barb had tried, I think—if I'm fair—to make an hour or so a little different from every other hour of every other day. But Serge had clearly gone out of his way to make Selina's birthday very special, and I had a keen sense of being an unwitting party to a violation of that specialness.

I walked up their driveway just a moment or two after they had arrived back from somewhere. Serge was getting some parcels out of the trunk of the car, and Selina was standing beside the car reading a letter she had just opened. They hadn't passed me, so I figured they must have come from Peterborough, arriving via the back of the subdivision. Selina saw me first: she looked up from her letter and smiled at me. "Serge," she said quietly, and Serge turned around. His face was neutral—neither welcoming nor hostile.

"I've come to say I'm sorry," I said. "My mother ... drinks.

When she drinks, she says ugly things. I'm so, so sorry to have ruined Selina's birthday."

There was a moment, just a moment, when I feared that Serge was going to send me away. But he didn't. He looked at my miserable face, saw, perhaps, that my hands were shaking a little, and he opened his arms wide. "Charlie," he said. "Come here."

I went to him, and buried my head in his shoulder. Selina came around the car and began to rub my back. What did I do? I burst into tears. I'd never before, in my conscious memory, been held, affectionately, by a man, and his warm embrace, coupled with Selina's touch—his cologne, her perfume—felt *right* in a way that few things had ever felt right in my life. I didn't *think* it then, but I must have *felt*, blindly, inarticulately, *this is what it means to be forgiven and loved.*

"There, there," said Serge. "There, there, Charlie. Selina and I are not in the least angry with you. Are we, Selina?"

"No, no," said Selina, continuing gently to rub my back.

"We don't choose our parents," said Serge. "And your mother ... she had a bad night, that's all."

"No," I said, desperate to confess the depths of my family's ignominy. "She's always like that."

"But she cares for you, Charlie," said Serge. "Her concern for you was simply *distorted* by the alcohol. We don't judge, Selina and I. We don't judge."

"We all make mistakes," said Selina soothingly, now resting her hand on my shoulders. "Every one of us. It's part of being human." She nestled in next to me so that the three of us stood together, she and I in Serge's warm embrace.

I pulled back a little to look at both of them, and to seize the opportunity to sniff and wipe my nose, which was threatening to drip on Serge's neck. "You are just *so good*, both of you," I said.

Selina laughed a little, very softly. "No, no, Charlie," she said. "We've seen something of the world, that's all. We know not to rush to judgement."

"And you will learn that, too," said Serge, handing me a handkerchief. (I wasn't carrying Kleenex, and he'd recognized my distress.)

"Now, come inside and have some coffee. Coffee and brown toast," said Selina. "What do you think, Serge?"

"Coffee and brown toast is excellent," said Serge. "With some apricot jam." And yet again, I was a guest at their table. By the end of that morning I felt that the Boormans and I were fully reconciled, and that the damage of the previous evening had been wholly undone.

The following Saturday morning, I found myself with Randy, again walking through the fields to the north of the village. Remembering the black dog, I was carrying a walking stick that one of Barb's boyfriends had used for a time after he'd twisted his ankle at work—an accident he'd parlayed into a claim against workman's compensation that saw him paid something close to his full salary for fifteen months. Randy had gone me one better: he was wielding a machete, something you could bear legally in those days, though the police might have asked him a few questions if they'd seen him with it on the street. We felt fortified, then—armed against threats concretely canine and nebulously human. Randy was animated—for Randy: he had a proposal for me. "My dad says he'll pay us six bucks an hour," he said.

"That's not bad," I said, impressed despite myself. Six dollars was far above the minimum wage.

"You're damn right that's not bad!" said Randy, sounding aggrieved. "When was the last time you earned that much?"

"But it's hard work," I said. I hadn't done much real labour, and part of me worried that I wouldn't be up to it.

"Yeah, but we're only looking at five hours," he replied. "Thirty bucks for five hours work." I'd already done the calculation, and I was equally impressed: thirty bucks would buy a number of books and chocolate bars. It might even buy me a couple of new skin magazines—my old ones were very familiar by now.

I pretended to consider for a moment—but only for a moment. "Okay," I said. "When?"

"Tomorrow," said Randy. "Sunday. Eleven to four. We can have a beer or two after."

"'Kay," I said. Randy's dad probably *would* let us have a beer or two. He wouldn't put them into our hands, but he'd take them out of the case, look meaningfully at us, put them down somewhere, then leave. Randy thought his dad hung the moon. I wasn't so sure: Barb told he'd done time for break-and-enter when he was younger, and he often had alcohol on his breath, no matter what the time of day, when I visited. But at least he was *there*. He wasn't an abstraction.

"God, I wish I had a car," said Randy, swinging his machete viciously and lopping the heads off several wildflowers.

"I don't," I said.

"You don't?" he said incredulously, turning to look at me.

"Humans were meant to be walkers," I said, remembering what Serge had told me. "It's our natural condition." I quickened my pace just a little and looked ahead with great seriousness, as if we were just embarking on some continent-wide walkabout.

Randy's incredulity turned to disgust. "You're really weird sometimes—you know that?" he said.

Later that day, back at my home, I watched *Bewitched* on television. Of course, I was much too old for it, but I had a crush on Elizabeth Montgomery, the actress who played the witch. My Saturday afternoon ritual began with me making myself some jam toast and sugary tea, then sitting down to watch *Bewitched* and *Get Smart*. The phone rang and Barb, who was washing dishes in the kitchen, dried off her hands on the dish towel and picked up the receiver. "Hello?" she said, then: "No, he's not here. Who's this?"

"I *am* here!" I shouted. She knew damn well I was home.

"Hang on," Barb said, "I hear him now. He's just coming in." I went into the kitchen and reached for the phone. "It's your rich Jew friends," she said, not bothering to cover the mouthpiece.

"They're not Jewish," I said, glaring at her. "Hi. Hi, Selina."

"Bait girl," said Barb, back over by the sink. My mother wasn't a witty woman, but she could convey a wealth of meaning with a phrase or two. I was growing weary of it.

Selina's voice was clear, girlish, and warm: "Charlie, Serge and I are planning a picnic down by the river on Sunday. Would you like to come with us?"

"I'd love to," I said. "When?" But my heart fell at the answer. "I can't," I said. "I'd really like to, but I promised Randy I'd help him and his dad clear some brush on Sunday. Can I come with you some other time? I love picnics." Not that I'd ever been on one.

"Kimono-Fag will be really sad to hear that you can't come on his little picnic," Barb said when I'd hung up the phone.

"I'm not listening to you," I said. "I'm not listening to a word you say." But I was gravely disappointed, and found that I was fighting tears as I walked back into the living room and plunked myself back in front of the television.

"Do you want some supper?" Barb called. Her voice wasn't gentle, but it was an offer—an unusual offer. It was probably as close to a peace overture as she could come.

"I'll make myself something," I replied, my stomach full of toast and bitterness.

"Whose groceries will you use?" she rasped at me, angry that her kindness had been rebuffed.

"The government's," I said. And those were the last words we exchanged that day.

On Sunday morning, at about 10:40, I set out for Randy's house. He lived on the opposite end of town from the Boormans—an old brick house fairly close to the highway, but with a long wooded backyard that reached all the way back to land protected by the local conservation authority because it flooded every few years. When I arrived, Randy was just coming out of the house and heading towards his dad's pickup.

"Where you going?" I asked.

"See if I can find a drugstore that's open on a Sunday," said Randy, breaking his stride just briefly.

"Why?"

"My dad's put his back out and he wants mega painkillers. All we've got is Aspirin." Randy's father had done himself a real injury in a snowmobile accident a few years before. I didn't know the details.

"So what about the brush-clearing?" I asked—a bit selfishly, maybe.

"It's gonna have to wait," said Randy. "Dad won't let us use the chainsaw without him being there." He climbed into the cab of the pickup. "You want to ride with me?"

"Will you drop me off on Dean's Road?" I said. I saw suddenly that the day need not be wasted. If I couldn't make some money, I could at least spend some time with my friends.

"How come?" asked Randy, pausing for a moment.

"Serge and Selina invited me to a picnic," I said. "If we're not working, I can go."

Randy looked at me intently for a moment. "Will there be sex?" he asked.

"Give me a break," I replied. "It's a picnic."

"Just him and his wife?" He was looking at me very closely.

"The maid will probably be there," I said. "Are you dropping me off?"

"I guess so," said Randy, with just a hint of reluctance. "Get in." I climbed into the shotgun seat and settled in, ignoring the seat belt. Randy shoved a Cat Stevens eight-track into the machine, and pulled out of the driveway.

We drove for a moment or two without talking, Randy focused on the road. Whatever else he may have been, he was a careful driver: his dad had instilled that in him. "My dad's really in pain," he said suddenly.

"What did he do?" I asked.

"Nothin' much," said Randy. "He was just reaching for one of my mom's vases, or somethin'. They're on top of the kitchen cupboards."

"Bummer," I said. Cat Stevens was singing "Moon Shadow." It was a song I really liked.

"Yeah," said Randy. We came to a stop sign, and he waited patiently for an elderly gentleman to cross the road. "You know what my dad says?" he added.

"About what?" I asked.

"About women," said Randy. He turned to look at me.

"No," I said—but I was interested. Randy's dad had been in the army after he was in jail, and I felt sure he knew things that might be useful to me someday. Besides, it was difficult to conceive of a more interesting subject.

"He says there are two kinds of women," said Randy. "There are the whores—and they're good to sleep with. And then there are the ones that make good mothers. And they're no good in bed."

I took this in without comment. I had nothing to check it against. But it made sense. It might be true.

"It's kinda weird that it works like that," said Randy.

I thought for a moment longer. "Do you think it's true?"

"Of course it's true!" said Randy, thoroughly annoyed. "My dad's been with lots of women." But I wondered about that split. I couldn't imagine Selina being anything other than a wonderful wife and mother, and I was sure she'd be good to sleep with. I suspected that life was a little more complicated than Randy's dad thought.

Six

I had a pretty good idea where Serge and Selina would be picnicking: it was a spot I'd told them about; somewhere I'd discovered in my solitary ramblings through the years. It would have been easy for me to go directly to the place, a small clearing in the woods, near a stream and a stone's throw from the river, but I did not do so. Instead, when once Randy had dropped me—"Cop a feel for me!" he shouted as he pulled away—I jumped the ditch, walked the path for a couple of minutes, and then, when I was still a good one hundred yards away, stepped off it, and crept forward among the trees and bushes, stopping every now and then to listen carefully.

Why? I don't think I entertained the hope that I would be able to spy on an orgy of some kind, but I thought that I might, if I were lucky, see Selina in an unguarded moment. Perhaps I might see her changing tops. Maybe, if I were stunningly lucky, I might catch a glimpse of her changing into her swimsuit. My pulse raced at the thought. And yet, at the same time, I felt badly about what I was doing. After all, these were my friends—and Selina had been stunningly kind to me.

I heard her singing before I saw her. Doubled over, and moving from tree to tree, I gravitated towards her voice. She had left the picnic area and ventured some way into the woods, following the course of the stream. When at last I saw her, she was sitting on the bank and slipping off her shoes. As I watched she stood, picked up her shoes, and stepped into the water. Hiking her skirt a little with her one free hand, she moved out into the middle of the stream, still singing. So this is what I saw: a slim, beautiful woman, bare-legged to her thighs, walking in a sunlit stream, trees to either side, and singing to herself. She was like a goddess.

Finishing her song, Selina continued walking for a moment or two, then, laughing as she encountered a bit of a dip in the stream and the water moved up to within an inch of her raised skirt, she returned to the bank and stepped out. She then—and my heart leapt—dropped her shoes, unbuttoned the long shirt she'd been wearing over her skirt, took it off (revealing a small, sheer brassiere), sat down, and used it to dry her feet.

Had she put her shirt back on then, what was to come might still have been averted. I would probably have watched her move on, waited a couple of minutes, then found my way back to the path and arrived at the clearing with every appearance of innocence. But Selina kept her shirt off. She stood up, slipped her shoes back on, then set out in the direction from which she'd come. I followed, a fair distance away, but close enough that I kept her in sight in spite of the brush; and I was not far behind when she stepped into the clearing and made her way towards Serge, who was lying flat on his back blowing smoke rings into the air. Selina went to him, and stood above him, a foot on either side of his waist.

"Hello, darling," said Serge. He smiled at her. His voice was warm: a husband greeting a beloved wife. A beautiful, sunny day. A picnic lunch on the horizon.

"Hello, Serge," said Selina, and she lowered her crotch onto his, putting her hands on the ground and leaning forward to kiss him at the same time. They kissed passionately for a moment, then Selina took her right hand off the ground, moved it to Serge's chest, traced a line from his chest down to his mid-section, and began to unzip his pants. I caught my breath. If his pants came off, so might her skirt.

"Not now, darling," said Serge. "Later."

"Why not now?" said Selina, pouting a little.

"The girl..." said Serge, gesturing vaguely towards the woods. He reached up and tucked a strand of wayward hair behind her right ear.

"What about the girl?" said Selina playfully. She passed her hand over his crotch, looking him in the eyes all the while.

"She puts me off a little," said Serge, but he did not move her hand away. His voice conveyed a mild distaste—not, certainly, for his wife; but for the nearness of Milly. For the *fact* of Milly.

Selina's body language and tone of voice changed: "I don't like her, then," she said petulantly.

"No, no, Selina," said Serge. "She's harmless. Let me call her to fix our coffee."

"All right," said Selina. She kissed him once more, then stood up. Serge raised himself into a sitting position and put his thumb and forefinger around her ankle. It looked to be a fond gesture. They smiled at each other.

"Milly!" called Serge. "Come!" His voice echoed just a little in the glade.

"That's right," said Selina, kneeling beside him and brushing a leaf off her bra.

"Hmm?" said Serge.

"She should be called like that," said Selina. "As if she were a little piggy. Soo-ey!"

Serge laughed. God help me, I stifled a laugh too, completely oblivious, in that instant, of how pathetic and pig-like I was myself. I shifted a little, redistributing my weight so that I would be able to stay crouched in the underbrush. I was still a little aroused from seeing Selina in her bra, and I found I was enjoying this unlicensed glimpse into the intimate life of these people I admired so much. Spying gave me the illusion of power.

Milly appeared from the other side of the clearing: I don't know where she'd been or what she'd been doing. "Yes, sir?" she said.

"We want some coffee, Milly," said Serge. "Before we eat our lunch." His tone was peremptory.

"Yes, sir," said Milly again. She went to a picnic hamper, which I now registered for the first time, removed a thermos and some cups and saucers, and began to make coffee, pouring the cream first. Selina watched her closely. Serge stared off into the distance, apparently uninterested.

"That's too much cream," said Selina suddenly. Her voice was sharp. It took me aback with its sharpness. It was a voice I'd never heard before.

"Oh, I am sorry," said Milly, and she took the cup into which she'd just poured cream and tipped a little of it out on the ground.

Selina stood up. "What are you doing?" she hissed.

"I am pouring some of it away," said Milly, clearly frightened. She was squatting near the hamper, and it seemed, just for a moment, as though she were trying to shrink into it.

"Don't be so wasteful," said Selina. "Haven't you any sense?" She took a threatening step towards the girl, her right hand raised as if she intended to strike.

"I am sorry," said Milly. "I did not know what else to do." She looked cornered, helpless.

"Do you see this, Serge?" said Selina. "The piggy has been wasteful."

"Dear, dear," said Serge, glancing over at Milly.

"Have you any idea what fresh cream costs?" said Selina to Milly. I was struck by how radically different she looked and sounded from the way she'd always behaved towards me. Only moments before, in the stream, she'd looked like a water nymph, a sexy sprite, a love goddess. The transformation was extraordinary.

"I am sorry," said Milly again. "I was not thinking." The formality of her speech somehow added to her fragility, her vulnerability.

"That's not good enough," said Selina coldly.

"Please forgive me," said Milly. "I will be much more careful, I promise."

"The damage is done," said Selina. "Serge, what shall her punishment be?"

"Her punishment?" said Serge mildly. This time he allowed his glance to linger on Milly for a moment, before looking back at his wife.

"For wasting fresh cream," said Selina. "We need something appropriate."

"Oh, it's not worth the energy of punishing her," said Serge. "Let her prepare the cups more carefully, and we'll let it go this time." He began to check his pockets, looking, I suspected, for his silver cigarette case.

"This time," said Selina, then she turned to Milly: "You're lucky this afternoon," she said. "The master is merciful."

"Thank you," said Milly. She kept her eyes downcast.

"Tell him how grateful you are," said Selina.

"I am very grateful," said Milly. "Very, very grateful." And she dipped her head, making a kind of bow.

"Now," said Selina. "I'm watching every move you make." She sat down again.

Every move you make. Do you remember the Police song with that lyric? It wasn't a love song. Milly continued preparing the coffee, and did so without further misadventure. She stood and brought the two cups over to Serge and Selina, proffering them with her eyes fixed on the crockery.

"Just put them down there," said Serge, nodding curtly at the ground.

"And put those containers back in the hamper," said Selina. Milly did as she was told. As the girl put the cream and the sugar away, Selina reached for her coffee cup, raised it to her lips, and took a sip. "Oh!" she said in apparent disgust—and she spat the coffee out.

"What is it, my darling?" said Serge, looking genuinely alarmed.

"This coffee is cold," said Selina. She said it in the same way you or I might declare that someone had dribbled into our soup.

"Cold?" said Serge.

"It's undrinkable!" said Selina.

"I am sorry, ma'am," said Milly. "It was hot when I put it in the thermos!" There was a note of desperation in her voice.

"It was hot when you put it in, was it?" said Selina. "Well, then, something you did *after* you put it in made it cold. Did you put the top on immediately?"

"Yes!" cried Milly.

"What?" said Selina.

"Yes! Yes, I did put the top on immediately," said Milly. She had begun to cry. "I was very careful, ma'am. I swear I was."

"Serge," said Selina. "This has ruined our picnic." She looked ugly: there's no other word for it. Ugly with anger. She looked utterly unlike the woman I knew and loved. I saw, in that instant, that she and my mother had more in common than I would ever have dreamed.

"Oh, my love..." said Serge.

"No, the picnic is ruined for me," said Selina. "This cold, useless coffee has spoiled what should have been a beautiful occasion. This, this *pig*, has corrupted our afternoon together."

"I'll make it up to you, darling," said Serge, and he moved a hand to Selina's back and began to rub gently. Just for a moment, it appeared that things might end there: Selina closed her eyes and seemed about to surrender to his touch. I was hoping that it might be so, almost praying that the storm would pass and that the glimpse I'd had of a harridan had been a terrible mistake, a grotesque aberration.

"No," she said suddenly, opening her eyes. "It's not you who needs to make amends, Serge. It's this *animal*. It's this *thing*." She stood up. "Come to me, piggy-thing!" she cried.

Milly rose and retreated a step or two. "Please, ma'am—" she said.

Selina sprang forward and seized Milly from behind as she turned to flee. "Got you! Got you, you piggy-thing!" she said.

"Please let me go, ma'am," said Milly. "I'll do anything—"

"Look, Serge," said Selina. She twisted Milly around, then forced her to kneel facing him; she then pushed the girl's chest forward by pulling her arms back and digging her knee into the small of the younger woman's back.

"Yes, I see, Selina," said Serge. He looked at Milly coolly, appraisingly, his eyes hooded.

"Would you like to see more?" asked Selina. A playful note had crept into her voice, but it was the playfulness of a cat with a tiny field mouse. I could scarcely believe what she was saying—but my body responded.

"Hmm?" said Serge. But in the next few seconds he clearly made a decision. He took a last draw on his cigarette, then stubbed it out on the ground.

"Please..." said Milly, weeping. "Please, no." She struggled, but to no avail.

"Shut up, you *piggy-thing*," said Selina. "Just shut up." Holding Milly's thin wrists with one hand, Selina reached around to the girl's front and ripped at her blouse, revealing her small breasts. "Look. Look, Serge," she said.

"Well," said Serge. "Well, this is most interesting. I think I could..." He rose and went over to Milly and Selina. Selina sank to her knees and pulled Milly backwards, pinning her arms behind her back in the process. Serge looked at Milly for a moment, then began unzipping himself as he sank to his own knees. He reached under Milly's skirt, pulled off her underwear, and raped her, climaxing after just a few vicious thrusts. When his spasms had finished, Selina let go of Milly. The girl lay immobile, squashed between the two of them. Selina stroked Serge's hair.

"Was that good, Serge?" asked Selina. She was breathing hard.

There was a brief silence as Serge collected his thoughts. "That was good," he said finally.

"You looked powerful. You looked like a man," said Selina.

"Thank you," said Serge. He reached down and zipped himself back up, then rose and went to the picnic hamper, straightening his clothes as he walked. He rummaged through the hamper and took out a bottle of mineral water. He unscrewed the top, put the bottle to his lips, and drank. Selina watched his every movement. Milly wept quietly. "It's good to vary things a little," Serge said reflectively.

At this, Selina pushed Milly off her, contorting her face as she did so. Milly curled up in the foetal position on the grass. "Slut!" said Selina. "Asian slut!"

"Selina," said Serge. His voice was mild, the tone one of gentle reproach.

"I'm sorry, darling," said Selina, standing up and brushing herself off. "But she disgusts me so. Filipino filth."

"I understand that disgust," said Serge. "But we must never compromise our standards. Hmm?" He cocked his head and smiled at his wife. There was a pause. Selina relaxed a little.

"I'm sorry, Serge," she said. "I was just upset about the coffee."

"Come," said Serge gently. Selina went to him, and he wrapped one arm around her. "We are not as others are," he said.

"No, Serge," said Selina. Her lips parted as she gazed up at him.

"So. Soil these pretty lips no longer," said Serge. He brought his finger to her lips and stroked them. She closed her eyes. There was a quiet moment between them. Milly continued to weep, silently, on the grass. At length, Serge turned his attention to her. "Take a few minutes to pull yourself together, girl. Selina and I are going for a walk. We'll have lunch in twenty minutes."

Milly gave no sign that she had heard, but Serge clearly assumed that she had. He and Selina went off together, down a path that went deeper into the woods. Selina leaned against him as they walked. Two hawks wheeled overhead.

And what of me? How was I left? When Serge and Selina passed out of sight, I turned from the scene and sat down on the ground, amidst the leaves and dirt. I was at once appalled and, God help me, aroused. "Jesus," I said. "Jesus, Jesus, Jesus." It wasn't a prayer.

Barb was sitting at the kitchen table, smoking and scanning the local newspaper's advertising supplements, when I came in. The radio was playing country music. I went to the fridge, took out a can of pop, and struggled to pull off the tab—but my hand was trembling too much.

"Where've you been?" asked Barb.

"Out," I said.

She noticed my hands shaking, and for all I know saw other signs of disorder, too. "What's wrong with you?" she asked.

"Nothing," I said, hastily leaving the kitchen. I didn't want to talk about this with Barb. I didn't know what to do with myself.

"That's no way to speak to me," said Barb. "Hey! I said that's no way to speak to me!" But I was gone.

I rushed upstairs to my room, and slammed the door behind me. My mind was filled with a welter of images. There was horror in those images—real horror—and the soundtrack I kept hearing was Selina's voice saying, over and over again, "you *piggy-thing*, you"; but there were other kinds of images, too—Milly's breasts, Milly's bare legs—and the horrific and the erotic somehow combined in a fearsome, loathsome, *toxic* brew. In that moment, in the summer I was seventeen, I threw myself down on my bed and unzipped my own pants. A dark and fetid eroticism prevailed.

I suppose I must have slept for a little while. The next thing I remember was hearing voices, familiar voices, coming to me as if from a dream. "He's bein' a real asshole," I heard Barb say, and Randy's response: "That's his job right now, Mrs. K." It took me a moment to realize that the tread of feet on the stairs signalled someone's arrival. I was scrambling up when a knock sounded on the door, and struggling to put myself back together when the door opened. Fortunately, the room was quite dark. "Go away," I said.

"Relax," said Randy, coming in. "It's not your mom. Whatcha doin'?"

"Nothing," I said.

"So what's up?" Randy asked, looking at me shrewdly, his

gaze taking in the rumpled bed, the untucked shirt, my clear embarrassment.

"Nothing's up," I said, all too aware of the pile of Kleenex beside the bed.

"Not any longer, hey?" said Randy. He didn't miss much.

"Give me a break," I said, and I sat down on the bed, overwhelmed suddenly by a flood of vivid images and disturbing memories.

"What's the problem?" asked Randy. There was concern in his voice—just a little: we'd known each other a while.

"There's no problem," I said. But I wanted to tell him. I wanted to tell somebody. I couldn't keep such a thing absolutely to myself.

"So how was the picnic thing?" he asked.

"I didn't go. Not exactly." I discovered that my chin was wobbling.

"What d'ya mean, *not exactly*?" He sat down on a beanbag chair in the corner of my room.

"I went to the place, but I didn't ... come out." I didn't know how to approach it.

"What?" said Randy.

"I ... saw something," I said. "Something I wasn't supposed to see." My hands wouldn't keep still. I brought them to my chin, then let them fall and rest on my knees.

There was a pause—or maybe there wasn't: maybe my memory is just supplying one. "So? What *did* ya see?" asked Randy.

How do you answer that? How do you answer when you've witnessed a rape, but there are spent Kleenex at your feet? How do you find the words to convey that you saw a great wrong, but were somehow, weirdly, *wickedly* excited by it? How do you find the words to express your abject confusion? "They did things with her," I said.

"Who did things with her?" said Randy.

"Serge and Selina. My friends." Their faces swam into my head —Selina, her face twisted in anger; Serge, climaxing. And Milly's face was in there, too—tears in her eyes, her mouth open as she cried out, her fists clenched helplessly at her sides.

"Did things with who?"

"With Milly."

"The maid?"

"Yeah."

"Sex things?" asked Randy. And the excited look on his face told me he was the wrong person to tell ... but I had no one else.

"Yes," I said.

"Did you get in on the action?"

"No!"

"Why not?" Genuine bewilderment. The same response as if I'd walked past a $20 bill lying unclaimed on the sidewalk.

"She didn't want it," I said.

"She didn't want you?"

"She didn't want anyone. She didn't want to..."

"You mean they *raped* her? They *raped* their maid?" Randy leaned forward, his eyes wide.

I paused. I really did. This was the first time the word had been said aloud. "Yeah," I said.

"Cool," said Randy—and he licked his lips.

"No. No, it wasn't," I said. "It was ... weird."

"She had to be asking for it, though, eh?" said Randy. "I mean, she's a Chink, isn't she? They all want it, you know."

"She didn't want it," I said, shaking my head.

"Come on," said Randy. "I bet she got into it." His face was twisted up again. I saw the hunger there—the untamed, wild-eyed, brutish lust. *What are women for if not this?* it said. *And if the women of our own kind are too well-defended, bring on the women of other tribes.* I knew that voice. It hissed and snarled and yelped in my head, too.

"No," I said, and I looked at the floor as my memory, unbidden, conjured up the actual moment of the rape: Serge thrusting, Milly crying out, the cruel expression on Selina's face.

"Did they go all the way?" asked Randy.

"Yeah," I said.

"Did you see everything?"

"Yes!" I said—exasperated, angry, lost.

"All right, all right," said Randy. "But I don't see why you're bent out of shape over this. I mean, you saw some broad getting laid. Big deal. Big hairy deal."

"It didn't feel right," I said.

"And that's why you're home jerking off?"

He had me. I had no truthful defence. "I wasn't jerking off!" I said.

Randy didn't challenge me. "Look," he said, "This is simple. You saw the maid getting laid.—The wife got into it, too?"

"She held her arms," I said.

"I wish I'd been there," said Randy. "But there's no problem. There's no problem, Charlie—except that you didn't get any this time."

"What do you mean?" I said.

"This isn't rocket science, Charlie," said Randy. "They're *your* friends, right? And she's *their* maid?"

"Yeah." I saw where this was going. And Milly's nakedness had aroused me. And before—at the Boormans' house—I'd noticed the sway in her hips. And hadn't she worn that provocative yellow dress, and the black stockings, and the high heels? And hadn't she let Serge caress her buttocks?

"So you're entitled, too." He flipped his hair out of his face and looked straight at me.

"It didn't feel right," I said lamely.

"I bet *she* felt all right," said Randy.

"She was crying," I said.

"That's not what I meant," said Randy. "I bet she *felt* pretty good, Charlie. You know what I mean?" I knew what he meant. We looked at each other, Randy and I, for about half a minute—probably the longest either of us had met the eyes of another boy in our lives thus far. And what passed between us? I don't know. I loathed him—hated what he was saying—but also, at some level, I saw he was just like me, and I was just like him. The chief difference between us came down to this: I was ashamed of the reptile flicking its tongue in my psyche, while Randy wanted to take his for a walk and show it off.

My friend left a couple of minutes later. I heard him clomping down the stairs, and Barb intercepting him at the bottom. "What's he doing?" she asked.

"He's goin' to bed," Randy answered.

"He's going to bed!" exclaimed Barb. "Is he sick?"

"No, just tired," said Randy, opening the front door.

"What happened to him?" asked Barb. She clearly had no idea.

"You'll have to ask him, Mrs. K," said Randy, and the door closed behind him.

"I don't need this shit," my mother muttered. And then, "I don't need this shit!" she shouted up the stairs. I just lay on my bed, staring at the ceiling. I thought about the things I'd seen and heard that day. I wondered what kind of people Serge and Selina really were. I thought about Randy, and the things he'd said. I thought about Milly, and the black stockings she'd worn on Selina's birthday, and her naked breasts at the picnic. I wished I had a dad like Mr. Boone. I wished my mother stayed home nights. I wished we had a big house and a beautiful garden and a swimming pool. I wished that some gorgeous young woman would take me into her heart and between her legs. My eyes blinked, then blinked again ... then closed. Sleep has ever been my refuge from shock.

But while I slept, my sleep was anything but peaceful. I found myself in a nightclub, and there was sexy, slow-dance music playing. Milly entered and began to writhe and gyrate to the music. Then Serge came in: he went over to Milly and ran his hand from her belly down and under her skirt. He produced something from between her legs. "Come and see what I have for you, Charlie," he said.

I went over to him, and Serge suddenly produced a snake—a dead snake. He took it between his thumb and forefinger and made it straight and stiff, then put it between his own legs, turning it into a long, demonic phallus. He laughed, and offered it to me. "For you, Charlie," he said.

"How much do you want for it?" I asked. It seemed a perfectly natural question.

"It's free," he said. The lights from the disco ball played over his face, and the music swelled louder.

"Free?" I said. "Are you sure?"

"Of course I'm sure," he said. "And you can do with it what you like." He gestured towards Milly, who was now standing meekly at his side. "Go ahead," he said. "Be my guest. Take her any way you like." And he laughed again, then disappeared.

I held out the snake to Milly. Milly sank to her knees, raised her head, opened her lips—and then suddenly it wasn't Milly at all, but Selina! I jumped back. Selina's face contorted into an ugly mask. "Take me, *piggy-boy!*" she said.

I woke up in a cold sweat, and looked wildly around my bedroom. Spotting the plastic garbage bin near the bed I dove towards it, and spent the next two minutes vomiting, then just retching. But I could not get rid of the images in my head so easily.

Just outside the village of Marmora, in eastern Ontario, there's a great big, ugly hole in the earth—the biggest I've ever seen. It's a quarry, the Marmora quarry. Once, in my late thirties, I was driving from Peterborough to Ottawa, and I stopped there to stretch my legs and just stare down into the pit from a viewing platform. My ex-wife had taken a cultural studies course at a nearby university while we were still married, and the professor had arranged a field trip to come see this thing. She had raved about it for weeks afterwards, describing it as awe-inspiring and a monument to nihilism, and while I'd not visited it then, despite her encouragement, I felt I owed it to the ashes of our marriage to see what she'd been so worked up about. I parked my car, made my way through the monster tires that served as a kind of barrier, and found a biker—a gang member—already enjoying the view.

"Fuckin' amazin', eh?" said the biker, by way of greeting.

"It's certainly a big hole," I agreed.

"Biggest goddamn pisspot in the world. I stop here whenever I'm drivin' by." And my tattooed friend unzipped himself, and urinated defiantly into the pit.

"There's a woman I think you should meet," I said.
"Eh?" said the biker.
"A woman," I said. "I'll give you her phone number."
"She like this place, too?" said the biker.
"She thinks it's fucking amazing," I said, a little sadly.
And why do I tell this little anecdote now? Because sometimes, when a speaker needs to deliver some bad news, he begins with a joke. The alternative, of course, is to jump right in. I was about to jump into my own personal abyss.

Seven

I slept until 9:30 the next morning. When I went downstairs, Barb was eating a bowl of cereal at the kitchen table: she watched me carefully. I went to the fridge.

"Bait girl called again," she said.

"Mrs. Boorman," I said, pouring myself a glass of milk.

"Whatever," said Barb. "She wants me to tell you that you're welcome for a swim. This afternoon." She slurped her cereal milk.

"Okay," I said. I looked out the window at the robin's nest. The babies all had their beaks open and pointing straight upward, but the mother was nowhere in sight.

"So what guy stuff were you and Randy talking about yesterday?" Barb asked with studied casualness.

"Oh, he's got the hots for Susan Ashe," I said. The milk tasted a little off, but I finished it anyway. I knew from my biology course that it wouldn't hurt me.

"That's not what you were upset about," said Barb shrewdly.

"I was pissed off," I said, looking down at my feet. "I was supposed to make some money yesterday working for Randy's dad, but he hurt his back."

Barb bought it—or seemed to. "Maybe you could offer to cut Mrs. Crossley's grass," she said. Mrs. Crossley was a neighbour four doors down. She was very proud of her geraniums.

"Maybe I will," I said. I rinsed out my glass and put it into the rack.

"Aren't you going to have something to eat?" asked Barb. It was unusual for her to be so solicitous.

"I'm not hungry," I said. It was true. The pictures were back in my head, and my stomach was feeling rebellious again.

So I went to church—or, to be more accurate, I went to visit a church. There was a little United church just two blocks from my home, and I knew that at least two of my teachers attended there, and a few kids from the high school were in some sort of youth group, too. Of course, it wasn't Sunday, but I had an idea that the minister might be there, and might be willing to talk with me. I walked up the short path to the door, rehearsing the things I would say to start a conversation ... but the door was locked. I went round the side to see if the door to the church hall might be open, but it was locked, too. I stood there irresolutely for a moment or two, then knocked; as I was standing there, however, I saw Roger's pickup pull over.

"Hey, Charlie!" Roger called. He was leaning over the passenger seat to look at me.

"Hi, Roger," I called back.

"What you doin'?" he said. His expression showed his surprise at seeing me there. You always knew what Roger was thinking: his face was an open book.

I gave up on the church. It was clear no one was going to answer. "I was just curious," I said, approaching Roger's pickup. "I've never been inside one of them."

"Locked, eh?" said Roger. He turned and spat out the driver's window.

"Yeah," I said.

"Want a ride to your place?"

"I've just come from—" I began, but then I realized I needed to collect my swimsuit if I was going to the Boormans'. I climbed inside the cab. Roger pulled away. I looked at his profile for a moment, and briefly considered confiding in him. He cared about my mom, didn't he? Who knew, he might have something to say that would somehow help. But as I was beginning to fumble for the words that might open a door, Roger leaned forward and turned up the radio. The cab was suddenly full of country music, and there was no space left for confidences.

Sears catalogues. Eaton's catalogues. Those were my introduction to the half-clad female form. I used to drool over the lingerie ads. And every now and then there'd be an advertisement in a mainstream magazine that showed a woman naked from behind: you couldn't see much, but the picture was an aching reminder of the marvels of the female form. If you couldn't afford a skin magazine—and skin magazines weren't cheap—these were the things that fed your fantasy life in those days. Unless, of course, you got lucky, one way or another. At seventeen, I hadn't got lucky. Hadn't even come close.

And then, of course, there was my mother. Sometimes Barb didn't wear much around the house. And sometimes, when there wasn't a man in her life, she'd get drunk at home, and when she got drunk she could be pretty casual about how she wore what little she did wear.

One night, when I was thirteen or fourteen, I woke up well after midnight and couldn't get back to sleep. The television was on downstairs, and I figured Barb had forgotten to turn it off. Resolving to fetch myself a bowl of cereal and turn off the set, I descended the stairs.

My mother was awake, however; she was sitting on the sofa and pouring herself a glass of bourbon when I came in. She wasn't smoking at that instant, but the air was stale with cigarette smoke. And though she was wearing a robe, it wasn't tied shut, so I got an eyeful of her bare breasts and sheer bikini panties. She was very, very drunk.

"Mom!" I said, and I froze.

Barb was too far gone to say anything coherent. She gave me a kind of dismissive wave, as if she were shooing away a housefly, then put her glass to her lips and took a deep gulp of bourbon. She was drinking it neat, but it might as well have been water.

She was watching a late night showing of *The King and I* —the 1956 version with Yul Brynner and Deborah Kerr. Less than a minute after I came into the room, the two actors began to dance. My mother watched for a moment, then put her glass down and rose unsteadily to her feet. She started to waltz to the music, solo, lost, completely lost, in the magic of a mythical Thailand. And as she danced, her robe fell off her shoulders, and I could see, as plainly as if I were in a strip club, her breasts, her nipples, her still taut stomach, her all-but-naked pubis. And I was fascinated. I just stared.

When the dance ended, Barb stopped dancing too and stood, swaying, eyes closed, in the middle of our small living room. I took one last look at her nakedness, then went back upstairs, my bowl of cereal forgotten. I was as aroused as I'd ever been in my life.

Back in my room, I sat down on my bed and stared at the wall. I was stiff, yes, and my pulse was racing, but I was also deeply conflicted by what I'd seen and how I'd responded. Barb was my mother—and I desperately wanted her to be the kind of mother to me that other mothers were to their sons and daughters. But Barb had never acted much like a mother: she was either tough (to me) or a coquette (in the early stages of her relationships with men), and the truth is she was still, at thirty-four or so, a very attractive woman.

So the first naked woman I ever saw, in the flesh, was my own mother, dancing. And I'm not trying to excuse myself for the thing I did, but I think it's one of the reasons I was so confused. It doesn't get me off the hook, I know; but surely it means something.

Milly opened the Boormans' front door at my knock. To every external appearance she seemed unchanged, but then she'd never seemed either the picture of health or confidence. "Hi, Milly," I said awkwardly.

"Hello, Mr. Charlie," she said. The fingers of her left hand fiddled with the top button of her dress, as if checking to make sure it was done up.

"How are you?" I asked.

"I'm fine. Thank you," she said. "Will you not come in?" I had been standing at the threshold.

"Where are...?" I said, stepping in. For some reason, I was loath to say *Serge* and *Selina*. It was absurd, but some vestige of delicacy in me felt that saying their names aloud, to her, would be a kind of offence—might reduce her to tears.

"They are by the pool," said Milly. "Would you like me to take you to them?" There were fresh flowers in the vase, I saw—flowers I did not recognize—and though they were beautiful, their perfume was heavy, almost sickly sweet.

"No," I said. "No, that's okay. I know the way." Milly smiled a small, tight smile, and turned to go. "Milly," I said.

"Yes?" said Milly, turning back to me.

"I'm sorry I wasn't able to make the picnic yesterday." I've no idea why I said it.

Milly said nothing: she just looked at me. I hesitated a moment, then left. I sensed that Milly remained standing where I left her, looking straight ahead.

Serge and Selina had set themselves up on the sunny side of the pool enclosure. They were both stretched out in lounge chairs, and both were wearing sunglasses (which weren't as common then as they are now). Serge was wearing his boxer-style swimsuit, while Selina was in the tiniest of bikinis—this one purple.

Selina saw me first. "Welcome, Charlie!" she cried, sitting up and waving.

"Welcome, my friend," said Serge. And with those two brief

speeches, the bulk of my angst receded, at least for the moment. Who else in my life said *welcome* to me? Who else called me *friend*?

"Come and give me a kiss," said Selina, offering me her cheek. I went to kiss her cheek but, as on her birthday, she gave me her lips instead. Her softness, her scent, her smile, banished the memory of her expression when—when what? Suddenly the brilliance of the present eclipsed all memories of the past.

"It's good to see you," said Serge. "Are you wearing your swim-suit under your shorts?"

"Yes. Yes, I am," I said, absurdly patting my hip.

"Strip off, then," said Serge. "Selina promises she'll close her eyes."

Selina laughed merrily, and did not close her eyes. She looked mostly at her husband, however, while I stepped away a few paces, removed my shirt and shorts, and folded them neatly. "We've been talking about taking a little holiday somewhere, Charlie," she said. "I want to visit the Scandinavian countries, but Serge is dreaming of South America."

"We've been to Europe so many times, my darling," said Serge.

"Where do you think we should go?" Selina asked, turning to me.

"I don't know," I said. "I've ... I've never been anywhere, really. For me, Toronto's a big deal." I was serious: I'd been to Toronto once. It had been a big deal. I'd spent two hours walking around Chinatown, my mouth open.

"But if you had a choice, Charlie," said Serge, "which would you choose: tired old Europe—or the wilds of Patagonia and the soaring mountains of Peru?"

Selina laughed again: "That's not fair, Serge. Charlie, the choice is between busty Swedish blondes, or huge guinea pigs."

"Well, if that's the case," I said, "I'd go with the blondes every time."

"That's called bribing the judge, Selina!" said Serge. "Penalty, penalty! If I had a red card, I'd wave it at you." And we all laughed, laughed yet again, as we'd done on scores of other occasions in our brief acquaintance. Indeed, our friendship seemed defined by easy, angst-free laughter.

It was just dying down when Selina hit me with her little bombshell. "So," she said, "do you think your mother will let you come with us?"

"Pardon?" I said. I really was several steps behind.

"Do you think your mother will let you come?" Selina was serious.

"My mother?" I said, bewildered. "Oh—we don't have the money, Selina. Mom's on welfare, you know. It's ... it's not possible. But thanks for thinking of me."

"The money is not a problem, Charlie," said Serge quietly. He was drinking a gin-and-tonic, and there was a book of detective stories by his chair.

"It is when you don't have it," I said, attempting a joke of my own.

But Serge interrupted me. "The money is not a problem," he repeated. "You would be our guest."

"Your guest!" I said, staggered.

"Our guest and our companion!" said Selina. "We feel so close to you, Charlie, that we would not dream of leaving you behind." The look on her face was absolutely earnest—almost childlike.

"I couldn't—" I began, but Serge interrupted again.

"A young man should see the world," he said. "It's an important part of his education. You need to meet people from other cultures, Charlie. You need to see different places and do different things." He was nodding as he spoke.

The phrase "different things" briefly gave me pause. It seemed clear, however, that Serge was talking about sightseeing tours and museum visits. "But the money!" I said. "You're talking about ... thousands. It's too much."

"Don't be silly," said Selina. "We have it! And what is money but a means to looking after the ones we care about and love? It would give us pleasure for you to come. You would be doing *us* the favour."

"It would be cruel of you not to come," said Serge. "I've been thinking, Selina, that maybe we should compromise on Chile and Argentina."

"Wrong hemisphere, Serge!" said Selina. "Try Germany and Austria."

"Hmm," said Serge. "Germany and Austria. Well, if we must go to Europe..."

"And we would look after the preparatory costs as well, Charlie," said Selina. "We'll need to get you a passport, and buy some decent luggage." Even in the midst of my wonderment at this idea, I saw that she filled her bikini top perfectly. Her breasts—

"Good luggage is very important," said Serge. "And comfortable travel clothes. And skis! We must all get new skis! We will go on a little shopping expedition."

"It's settled, then," said Selina. "Oh, I'm so glad!" She clapped her hands.

"I'll have to speak to my mom," I said, dazed at the way things had unfolded, but ready to embrace the possibility that something exciting might happen. Foreign travel wasn't something I'd ever even dreamed about, any more than I'd dreamed of visiting the moon.

"Of course," said Serge. "Actually, speaking of your mother, we have a small gift for her, Charlie."

"A kind of peace offering," said Selina. "Because we've been monopolizing you so much recently."

"Your mother has kept her figure wonderfully," said Serge, "and Selina saw a lovely dress the other day—"

"Oh, it's so beautiful," said Selina, drawing a sinuous line in the air as if to emphasize the elegance of the design.

"So we've wrapped it up nicely, and you can take it home to her after dinner. It may help her to look more kindly on your having an adventure with us." Nothing about Serge's tone or expression betrayed that this was effectively a bribe. Slow as I was in some ways, however, this seemed a remarkably well-planned stratagem on their part, and I wondered, if only briefly, what they could possibly expect of me in return.

"I'll get the package right now, before we forget," said Selina. And she stood up, and positively danced her way across the pool deck and into the house. Serge and I watched her go: no red-blooded man could have looked elsewhere.

There was an easy, comfortable silence between Serge and me—though my mind was, simultaneously, spinning. I was thinking that I had surely won a kind of lottery—some sort of celestial jackpot—but a question was beginning to take shape in my mind: *what had I done to deserve such largesse?* And if I hadn't already done it, whatever it was, *what would I need to do?* Serge took the opportunity of Selina's absence to take out his silver cigarette case and light a cigarette. "Your front crawl is getting better and better, Charlie," he said. "If you trained, you could swim competitively."

"I don't think I'm that good," I objected, but I was quietly pleased all the same.

"With practice, anything is possible," said Serge. "You have a good, strong body, and a clever brain: you can do anything you set your mind to."

"Thanks," I said. Serge opened up vistas in the same way that Mr. Boone did—but Mr. Boone had never offered to take me to Europe. Teachers didn't have the money to do that kind of thing. But when Mr. Boone crossed my mind, it occurred to me that he might be someone I could consult about this. He might be able to help me think things through.

"You will enjoy Germany," said Serge. "We'll take you down the Rhine. We'll see the Black Forest together. The castles, Charlie! And the beer gardens! And perhaps we'll venture into France as well. You cannot go to Europe and not see at least a little of France."

"I hope my mom agrees," I said, and a picture of Barb's disapproving face swam into my mind.

"I'm confident she will," said Serge. "She loves her son, and will want only the best for him."

"My mom's an odd lady," I said noncommittally.

Serge took a deep draw on his cigarette, then expelled the smoke in a long, elegant breath. "My friend," he said, "she is your mother and you must respect her. Respect her even when you don't understand her. I see much pain in her eyes."

"Well—" I said.

"Respect and love your mother, Charlie," said Serge earnestly.

"Whatever mistakes she makes, whatever grief she gives you, she has a good heart."

"Do you think so?" I asked, a little astonished at the thought.

"Yes. Yes, I do," said Serge. "Charlie, we can never really know what weight someone else is carrying. I sense that your mother is carrying a very heavy burden. She's not had much education, has she?"

"I don't think she even finished high school," I said. I knew she hadn't. She had grade eleven in the four-year stream, which meant she'd taken courses in things like hairdressing, typing, and home economics. I don't think she passed home economics.

"Exactly," said Serge. "And yet she is a clever woman. So one of the burdens she carries is frustration at not having opportunities she should have had. Think what she could have accomplished with a degree. Think how hard it must be for her to spend time with a succession of dull boyfriends."

I thought about that, and it made some sense. None of Barb's boyfriends had been rocket scientists. A couple of them had been to community college, but that was about the extent of it. And yet ... I tried to think of a time when my mother had expressed an interest in anything beyond herself. Was it possible that her self-absorption was the result of not knowing enough about the world?

"There is another dimension to this," said Serge, very seriously. "I think sometimes that we do not fully recognize the roles that different people are meant to play in our lives—not until years after the fact. I suspect that your mother sometimes seems a hard woman to you, Charlie, but perhaps her role is to toughen you up. Perhaps her gift to you is an emotional suit of armour. And perhaps other people in your life are charged with giving you gifts that are easier to carry."

At that moment, as if on cue, Selina returned, carrying a beautifully wrapped package. "Look what a pretty bow Selina has tied," said Serge.

Selina did a kind of mock curtsey: "Presentation is important," she said. "I'm surprised you're not in the pool, Charlie."

"We were both just going in," said Serge, stubbing out his

cigarette. "Come, Charlie!" And he seized my hand and, laughing—the both of us laughing—he pulled me to the side of the pool, and we jumped in together.

"Wait for me!" cried Selina. She put the package carefully on the third lounge chair, then ran to the side and dived in—arcing elegantly over Serge and me. There was an instant when she seemed almost to hover in mid-air—an athletic angel, a wingless bird—a lithe, graceful figure set against a light blue sky.

An hour later and we were fully clothed, if still a little wet-haired, and stretched out in the Boormans' living room. I was on one of the two couches, while Serge lay on the floor with his head in Selina's lap. We were listening to Wagner, because Serge felt I should begin to learn something about German culture in preparation for our trip. Milly entered with a tray and began silently to collect the used mugs and plates we'd generated in the course of eating a post-swim snack.

"I should go," I said, stirring myself as one piece of music ended.

"So soon?" asked Selina.

"Yeah," I said. "Thank you so much ... for everything." The truth was that being still, and listening to music, had started to stir things up in my mind again. I wasn't deeply unsettled, but I was beginning once more to see images as if in a series of filmed flashbacks. The difference, however, was that my mind had taken what I'd previously found disturbing—or mostly disturbing—and begun to transmute it into something almost attractive. Seeing Milly walk around the room; seeing her bend over once, twice ... I was a little aroused. It wasn't as simple as that, but arousal was certainly part of what I felt.

"Don't forget your mother's gift," said Serge, sitting up.

"No, I won't," I said. "But there's no need to get up, Serge."

"I'll just see you to the door," said Serge, beginning to rise.

"No, no need," I said. "I'll go with Milly."

Did Serge and Selina exchange brief glances? I'm not sure. Milly certainly paused on her way out of the room, and looked towards Selina. Serge laid his head in Selina's lap again.

"Kiss me, Charlie," said Selina, and I kissed her, collecting my prize from her lips without hesitation this time. I then picked up my mother's gift from the coffee table, where Serge had placed it on bringing it inside.

"Good-bye. Good-bye, Serge," I said.

"Good-bye, Charlie," said Serge, and he raised his arm in a kind of languid salute.

Milly turned to go, and I followed her out of the room.

As I followed Milly's slim figure down one hall, and then down another heading towards the front door, I found myself filled with contradictory feelings. On the one hand, I felt an enormous sympathy for this quiet, sweet, girlish young woman. Her vulnerability was self-evident, and I remembered too, and remembered vividly, the pain I'd seen etched in her face. On the other hand, I felt, what ... desire? Desire, yes, but even more a profound sense of entitlement. After all, if she was giving sexual pleasure to Serge and Selina, who were my best friends... If I formulated that sentence then, I doubt that I finished it; but I *felt* its conclusion—I knew where its logic took me. And you'd never think from the way she moved that she'd been hurt. No, it was clear that she was fine. Perhaps she'd forgotten it, or if not forgotten it ... *put it away* somewhere.

I made a decision—made it somewhere deep down below where I could see it being made. "Milly," I said.

"Yes, Mr. Charlie?" said Milly. We had arrived at the front entry hall, and she turned to face me. She looked, on the surface, impassive, but I read a guardedness in her eyes.

"Would you like to come for a walk with me tomorrow?"

"For a walk?"

"Yes," I said, doing my best to smile disarmingly.

"Where?" she asked. She was looking at me a little doubtfully, but she wasn't rejecting the idea. And I sensed, in holding her gaze a moment, how lonely she must have been, this woman of twenty-two, to even consider a walk with a callow seventeen-year-old.

"I don't know," I said. "In the woods, maybe. Or just through town. We could get an ice cream, or something. I'd buy."

"I do not know if Mr. and Mrs. Boorman would let me," said Milly. A shadow crossed her face.

"What if I asked them?" I said.

She paused. "All right," she said, still doubtful, but with a trace of animation.

"I'll phone them tomorrow," I said, pressing my advantage.

"All right," said Milly again.

"After dinner, then? While it's still light?" I said.

"Yes," said Milly. "Yes. Thank you."

"See you tomorrow, then," I said. And I smiled at her—more naturally this time. It's funny how easily deceit comes with a little practice.

"Good bye, Mr. Charlie," said Milly softly. She looked surprised, but pleased, too.

I let myself out.

I didn't go straight home, and when I eventually found my way to Reid Street it was getting on for 7:00. The Christian Nazi was banging on Donny's front door, but this time she was accompanied by someone else, an older gentleman, who stayed near the car and watched her with a trace of unease.

"Maybe you should just leave him be, Edith," he said, as I was passing. He was overdressed for a summer evening.

"No, Earl," she replied, pausing briefly in her banging. "The Lord wants me to do this for Donny." And then, calling out in a voice that could almost knock you over at close range: "Open up, Donny! We're taking you to see the fireworks!"

When I arrived home, Barb was cleaning up after her supper. She'd made sausages again, I judged from the smell: sausages and french-fried potatoes. It was a wonder to me that she remained so slim. I came into the kitchen and put the beautifully wrapped gift on the table.

"What's this?" asked Barb, her voice harsh and her expression suspicious.

"It's for you," I said.

"What is it?"

"It's a gift."

"A gift!" A girlish smile of pleasure lit up her face. Then: "Who from?" she said. Hard Barb was back in the house.

"Serge and Selina," I said.

"The fag and Mrs. Robinson, huh?" said Barb. "Why are they sending me a gift?"

"It's a peace offering," I said, and I patted the package gently.

"Yeah, right," said Barb. "What's the real reason?"

The fact that Hard Barb gave voice to my own deepest questions unsettled me a little. Had I somehow taken aboard her own cynicism, or was this something I needed to reflect on a little longer? I took a deep breath: "They want to take me to Europe."

"Why do they want to take *you* to Europe?" Her incredulity could not have been more clear.

"To show me the sights. For my company." It sounded thin even to my ears.

"Your naked ass is the one sight he's interested in," said Barb. But she said it almost by rote. She was eyeing the package with interest.

"You're wrong," I said. "He loves his wife." I lifted the package and held it out to her.

Barb dried her hands. "Give it to me," she said. I handed her the gift. Barb ripped it open. I flinched as she tore aside the ribbon and the expensive paper. Inside, however, was a beautiful red dress, and even my untutored eye told me it had cost a lot of money. Barb was impressed despite herself. "Huh," she said.

"It's nice, isn't it?" I said.

"The one good thing about fags is they know their fabrics," said Barb.

"Selina picked it out," I said.

Barb was silent for a moment: she was clearly having some sort of internal struggle. "But where am I going to wear this?" she said finally. "Hey? It's like giving me a crown—What's this?" She had noticed an envelope pinned to the hem of the dress. Opening it, she peered inside.

"What is it?" I asked.

"You don't know?" she said.

"No." In that instant, I had no idea.

"Never you mind, then," she said. "It's personal."

"Is it a letter?" I asked.

"It's personal," she repeated.

"Is it money?" I persisted.

"Shut it," she said. "It goes with the dress."

"So can I go to Europe?" I said. But I already knew what the answer would be. Barb was suborned.

Barb thought for a moment. "They're paying the shot?" She ran her fingers over the dress.

"Yes," I said.

"*Everything*?" She was just making sure.

"Everything," I said.

"Yeah, then. Yeah," said Barb. "Probably a good thing for you. Keep you out of trouble."

"And what about my naked ass?" I couldn't resist.

"Wear pyjamas," said Barb succinctly. "I'm gonna try this on."

That night, after I'd repaired to my room, I didn't immediately dig out either *Oliver Twist* or my skin magazines. No, my mind was on Europe. I was beginning—just beginning—to entertain the possibility that my life was changing in the way it might if I had indeed won a lottery. I'd gone by the small Greenfield library on my way home, and had taken out their one travel book on Germany. It wasn't a modern book—it was published in the 1930s—but there were enough maps and black-and-white pictures that I could lose myself for a while.

For an hour or two, then, I absorbed as much information as I could about Trier and Heidelberg and Cologne and Aachen; I read about the Rhine River castles, and about Oktoberfest and the Black Forest. I learned that the Black Forest is a wooded mountain range in southwest Germany; that its trees are predominantly pines and firs; that one can see eagles and owls in its skies and bears among its trees; that the Danube has its source there; and that it's famous for the manufacture of cuckoo clocks. I savoured these details. And I dreamed. I imagined myself on a tour boat; I imagined myself climbing steep staircases and looking out over ramparts; I imagined hoisting a stein in a beer garden and striding along a path in the Black Forest with a knapsack on my back. It was sweet to project myself into another world—a world where rich experiences were a kind of currency for the elect. It was sweet to think that I might become something other than Charlie of Greenfield, Barb Knowles's bastard. It was sweet to believe that I was someone whose company might be attractive to worldly people.

But if there was a kind of sweetness in this dreaming—and I think there was—sweetness wasn't the only savour in my soul that night. There came a time when I put aside the travel book and picked up the skin magazines. And I looked for one in particular, a magazine that featured a photoset with an Asian woman. And when I turned off the overhead light and turned on my bedside lamp and took myself in hand, it was easy to imagine that this young woman was Milly, and that her willingness, her boldness, was Milly's, too—the raw lust behind a façade of modesty. And when I came, and I came quickly, it was Milly's face I saw, in that instant, atop the pert breasts and parted thighs of the *Penthouse* model.

When I was six, Barb had a boyfriend who worked as a janitor at a Catholic high school. He was a good-looking guy, and fairly smart, and for a time Barb thought the two of them might make a go of it together. He was divorced with a couple of kids he never saw, and he and Barb talked about buying a fixer-upper in Peterborough.

I didn't mind the guy, but a couple of months after he and Barb started going out he looked after me one afternoon while my mom was visiting Edna. I was sitting on the bed in my room, reading, when he came in and sat down next to me. "What are you doing?" he asked.

"I'm reading this book," I said, angling the cover towards him.

"Show me," he said. He was sweating, I remember, and his hands shook a little when he took the book.

After a moment of looking at it distractedly, he set it aside and locked his eyes on me. "How you feeling?" he said.

"I dunno," I said. "I feel fine, I guess."

"You ever had a doctor do the *cough, kid* check-up?" he asked.

"No," I said. "What's that?"

"Stand up beside the bed," he said. So I did, and he suddenly grabbed my balls, though he didn't hold them very tightly. "Cough, kid," he said. So I coughed. "Again," he said. So I coughed again. For a moment, it looked as though he was going to ask me to do something else, but he didn't. "Okay," he said. "I guess you're healthy." He let go of me. He had an odd look in his eye, and I felt something wasn't quite right. His hands were shaking even more.

"How could you tell from doing that?" I asked. "Don't you have to take my temperature, or something? That's what Mom does."

"Nah," he said. "I can tell." And he left.

Later that day I told Barb that her boyfriend had done the *cough, kid* check-up on me to make sure that I was healthy. She asked a question or two, then her brow furrowed and she went very quiet. And that was the last I saw of him.

Eight

The evening after my library research I made my way to the Boormans' house through the fields, wielding the walking stick I'd taken to carrying since my encounter with the black dog. Usually, I simply waved it around—though from time to time, when I was sure I couldn't be seen, I'd pretend it was a sword and fence with an imaginary opponent. On this occasion, though, I caught myself whacking the heads off the wildflowers that grew by the path. I was in an odd, destructive mood.

That mood had, if anything, gathered force by the time I reached the vacant lot where I'd seen the Canada geese some days before. They were there again, though in a different part of the lot now. Their behaviour was much the same as it had been the last time: most of them seemed to be foraging, though for what I've no idea. They grazed, and they honked quietly to one another; two or three seemed to be sleeping. I stopped to look at them—but this time something about their passivity, their vulnerability, offended me:

moved to sudden anger, I waved my stick at them, and shouted—"Crazy birds! Useless shithogs! Get out of here! Get!" At this, most of the flock swiftly scuttled away, but I was impressed despite myself when a couple of geese actually stood their ground and hissed at me. I didn't stay to press the point, however. I had a date.

As I turned into the Boormans' driveway, my eye caught a glimpse of Milly peeping out the glass side panel of the front door. She was looking out for me. She was looking forward to my arrival. I felt, as I've so often felt, two very different things: a surge of anticipation ... and a kind of melancholy ache. Milly opened the door and slipped out as I drew nearer. We met in the middle of the drive.

"Hi," I said.

"Hi, Mr. Charlie." Her dress was, as usual, modest, but I thought I could discern a little makeup on her face: a trace of eyeshadow; a lick of lipstick.

"I'm glad you could come," I said.

"Me, too. Thank you for calling Mrs. Boorman. I do not get out much." She gave a small, shy smile. I helped her into a light summer jacket, discovering, in the process, that she'd washed with a lightly scented floral soap. Within her modest means, as I guessed them to be, she'd clearly done what she could to spruce herself up.

We began to walk together—not touching, but keeping fairly close. We passed a couple of blocks in something approaching silence: by this time we were leaving Hazelwood Estates, and would soon be moving into the fields that could take us either to the older section of town or, with a slight divergence, into the woods that bordered the river.

"Do you enjoy being a maid, Milly?" I asked. I felt I needed to say something. The silence felt more awkward than companionable.

"It is all right," said Milly, after a pause.

"You live in a nice house," I said. It was, of course, something more than nice; it could well have been the most opulent home in the village.

"Yes." Her answer was uninflected.

"Do you have a private room?" I asked.

"It is sometimes private." The absence of contractions aside, this answer struck me as a little odd. Did this mean that Serge visited her sometimes, I wondered. The idea both excited and unsettled me.

"That's important," I said.

"Why do you say that?" asked Milly. I was conscious of her looking at me, just for a moment.

"Well ... I like privacy. Don't you?"

Milly did not reply, but I sensed that she did not wish to talk further about her room. Her face had gone blank.

"Serge and Selina are taking me to Europe," I said.

"Are they?" Her voice was very quiet.

"Are you coming, too?" I asked. A car whipped by carrying two boys from my own grade. They stared at us. I felt a flush of pride at being seen in the company of a pretty woman.

"I do not know," said Milly. "I do not know what is happening to me." We left the road and started out on the path across the fields.

"Would you like to come? To Europe, I mean?"

"I do not know, Charlie."

"We're going to Germany," I said, babbling on. "Germany and Austria. We're taking a boat down the Rhine. Did you know that the Rhine is one of the longest rivers in Europe? It begins in the Alps."

"I am sure you will have a wonderful time," said Milly neutrally.

"Yeah," I said. "But doesn't the thought of going excite you, too?"

"One day I would like to go to Europe," said Milly. "But maybe not as a maid. Maybe not with Mr. and Mrs. Boorman."

"Oh," I said. "I can understand that." I speared a wildflower with my stick, but kept walking.

After a couple of minutes we came to that point where we needed to decide whether to proceed into town or to head towards the woods and the river. "Would you like an ice cream?" I asked.

"Maybe not right now," said Milly. "Unless you..." She looked at me again, as if she were trying to read my own wishes.

"No. No, I'm fine," I said. "Let's go this way, then." And we headed along the path that would take us into the woods.

Some years ago, in the midst of my marriage breaking up, I had real trouble sleeping, and my doctor put me on a pill that was supposed to help out. I reacted badly to the medication: I've never taken hard drugs, but when I read about bad acid trips, the description of what's involved resonates with me. I remember sitting in the middle of my living room and feeling that the walls were beginning to pulse inward. I remember looking down at my skin, and feeling sure that I could see it move—that something was crawling under the surface. In any event, I checked myself into a psychiatric facility, and stayed there nights for about a month, emerging only for ten hours a day to go to work.

I shared a room in the psychiatric ward with a fellow who had fried pretty well all his circuits on a pharmacy of psychedelic drugs. My nurse told me he had no memory—or very little. The one thing he did remember was a recording of Stephen Sondheim's "Into the Woods," and he used to sit on his bed, rocking back and forth, and singing, tunelessly, over and over, "Into the woods, into the woods, into the woods."

As an adult, I've grown to feel a passion about saving forests and other natural habitats, but I don't romanticize them, and I have no illusions about their having a mystically healing effect on sick humans. You find in the woods what you carry in with you—good and ill.

"It is a beautiful evening," said Milly, as we left the field and entered an area where spindly trees rapidly gave way to tall, mature ones. Her head was raised and her eyes were shining. I wondered how often she did get outside.

"Yeah. Yeah, it is," I said, deliberately looking away. I didn't want to look into her eyes. Not at that moment.

"The air is so fresh. Not like Toronto."

"Are you from Toronto?" I asked.

"I spent some time there," said Milly. "In my first job in Canada."

"I've only been twice," I said. "No, three times. No, twice." It had been just once. Why was it so important to lay claim to experiences I hadn't had? The woods closed around us, and we walked on in silence. I felt deeply unsettled, and I sensed that Milly had picked up on my agitation.

"Where are we walking?" asked Milly. She did not seem winded at all, though I was setting a fast pace.

"Oh, just along the path here," I said. In fact, we were heading, by a back route, towards the place where Serge and Selina had had their picnic.

"Could we go closer to the river?"

"We'd be more likely to see people," I said.

"I do not mind seeing people," said Milly.

"I'd really like more privacy," I said. "I'd like to get to know you better."

Milly stopped suddenly. "I really don't feel comfortable going in this direction," she said clearly. I saw that she was biting her lower lip, but there was resolve in the set of her shoulders.

"Oh, come on, Milly," I said. "I know a great place."

"A great place for what?" she asked. She was trembling a little, but her eyes remained on mine.

"For getting to know each other," I said. I could not look her in the eyes: I looked just above her right shoulder.

She put a slim hand on my shoulder. "Charlie," she said, "we are just going for a walk, are we not?"

"Yeah. Of course," I said.

"I do not want to neck, or anything." She made the word *neck* sound oddly formal.

"Who said anything about necking?" I said, doing my best impression of wounded innocence.

"I just want to be clear," said Milly. "You are a nice guy, but I just want to walk and talk."

"That's fine," I said, still unable to meet her eyes for more than a few seconds. "But let's go *this* way."

"I am trusting you, Charlie," Milly said. And given who her employers were, what choice did she have?

"'Kay," I said. I moved ahead and, after a brief pause, Milly followed me. We'd come to a muddy section of the trail. "The ground's a bit wet there," I said.

One summer, when I was in my early thirties, I spent some volunteer time with an ex-con. The idea was that you'd give the fellow the agency had chosen for you fifty minutes a week. You'd just sit and talk over a cup of coffee and a muffin. The challenge was to be constructive—to help your coffee buddy, as the director put it, "frame the difficult events in his life in a way that reduced his frustration and made his social reintegration more likely." You were encouraged to talk about your own frustrations, your own disappointments, and the constructive ways you'd handled them. I figured I could do that.

The fellow I counselled had served time for sexual assault. He was a man of reasonable height, six feet anyway, and he had a powerful chest and muscular arms. He told me that before he struck he'd feel an intense build-up of sexual tension—a tension he felt he could relieve only by taking what he wanted. "Was there any pleasure in it for you?" I asked.

He thought about that for a bit. "Yeah," he said finally. "But I hated myself, too, afterwards." I wondered if the qualification was true. I honestly don't know the answer.

We were now deep in the woods, and very near the spot where Serge and Selina had assaulted Milly: this was one of several clearings joined, loosely, by the narrow path we'd been following. "Here's good," I said.

"What for?" asked Milly.

"Stopping for a while," I said. I dropped my walking stick.

"I am happy to keep walking," said Milly. Her right hand fluttered a little.

"We need to stop," I said, rubbing my hands against my thighs.

"Why?"

I pumped up my bravado. "You know," I said. "You want it, too."

Milly went very still. "No, Charlie," she said. I noticed that she was again biting her lower lip.

"There's nothing wrong with having a man's feelings," I said. "And you're a woman."

"I do not want to neck, Charlie," Milly said.

"We don't have to *kiss*," I said.

"No, Charlie," said Milly.

"I have needs," I said. My voice had hardened and sounded rough even to my own ears. I was surprised by how strong I felt.

"No," she said. She could not have been more clear.

I hesitated, then grabbed her and wrestled her to the ground: she did not offer much resistance. I fondled her breasts roughly. She lay still. I was bigger, and stronger, and heavier. "Stop, Charlie," she said quietly. "Please."

"Take this off, will you?" I said harshly, trying without success to unbutton the back of her dress. The buttons were small and fiddly.

"Please stop," said Milly quietly. I continued groping her, frantically and joylessly. "Charlie," she said, "Stop. If it's love you want, this isn't how you get it."

I stopped. "What?" I said.

"It is love you want, yes?" she said. It was a question, but it was as if she knew the answer.

The words hit me like a Mack truck. Why? Because it was what I wanted. It really was. Beneath the aggression—beneath the pumped-up bravado, the darkness, the shit—yes, it was love that I wanted. I went very still. My desire, if it was desire, ebbed away. I had felt my cheeks hot and my pulse racing, but now that had passed and I was shaking.

"You are not a bad person, Charlie," Milly said. "That is not who you want to be."

I discovered, to my astonishment, that my eyes were wet and that I was shaking. "I don't want to be a bad person," I said. My voice broke.

"I know," she said quietly.

"Oh, God," I said. "Oh God, oh God, oh God." I was now shaking violently, and I lost all control of my face.

"Just hold me, Charlie," Milly said. "Gently."

I began to cry. I buried my head in her shoulder. "I'm sorry," I sobbed.

"I know. I know," she said.

"I'm so sorry," I said.

"I know," she said, and she stroked my hair gently. I wept for several minutes, my sobs at length losing their intensity, their desperation.

"Can you forgive me?" I asked.

"Yes. Yes, I do forgive you," she said.

We remained there for half an hour: I wept all the while, and she stroked my hair and stared up at the canopy of trees. But I realized, in that short time, that Milly was a person with a dignity and grace and selfhood of her own—that she wasn't merely an exotic sex toy, to be used and discarded. I had made a terrible mistake, certainly, but I had, I hoped, pulled back just before I plunged into an abyss of my own devising.

But yes, I know: that she should comfort *me* makes no sense at all.

When I woke the next morning, in my own bed, I stared at the ceiling for a long, long time. I wasn't sure what I should do; I wasn't sure where I should go. I felt sad and confused, but I didn't feel wicked. I didn't hate myself. I rose and showered. I put on clean clothes. I had some toast and jam and tea, and I decided to go for a walk. I was walking along Concession, not going anywhere in particular, when I heard Randy hailing me from behind.

"Hey, Charlie. Charlie! Wait up."

I waited. "Hi," I said, as he caught up. We walked together for a moment or two without saying anything.

"Well?" said Randy, unable to contain his curiosity any longer.

"Well, what?" I said. I'd left my stick in the forest, and my hands wanted something to do. I found that I was rotating my wrists and clenching my fists as I walked.

"Have you got some yet?" he asked.

I knew what he meant, but I didn't answer him immediately. "I don't know what I got," I said at last.

"What d'ya mean? Did she blow you?" he said.

"No," I replied.

"What, then? *What*?" Randy's eyes were wide—challenging.

"We talked," I said.

"You *talked*!" Randy couldn't believe his ears.

"Yeah," I said. "We had a conversation."

"Charlie, you are such a fuckin' loser sometimes. Where is she? I'll give her some fuckin' *conversation*."

I stopped walking and looked directly at Randy. "Don't touch her," I said.

"What?" He was stunned. Outraged. His eyes bulged.

"I said, don't touch her."

"Who's to stop me?" asked Randy. But he didn't move on me. I was bigger.

"*I'll* stop you," I said. I pressed my index finger lightly into his chest. It was the first time I'd asserted my greater strength, and it struck me that Randy and I would not be walking together again.

"You've fallen for her, haven't you?" said Randy. "You've fallen for the goddamn maid!"

"Just leave her alone," I said. "That's all."

"*Asshole*," said Randy. "You asshole."

"Whatever," I said.

Randy horked viciously, then spat in the dust beside us. He stalked off without looking back. An elderly lady was coming down the steps leading to her porch.

"That was a nasty thing to do, wasn't it?" she said.

"Yes, ma'am," I said quietly.

"I expect you were raised better than that," said the elderly lady.

"There's not much between us," I said. But I knew there was one difference.

Nine

I arrived home, much later, to find Barb wearing her new dress and admiring herself in a mirror in the front hall. She'd put on some makeup, too, I saw, and she smelled of a perfume I'd not smelled before —something much more subtle than her usual musk-laden scent. Barb's skin was too leathery and her face too sullen for her to be judged pretty, but she looked better than I'd seen her look in a long time. "What d'ya think?" she asked.

"It's nice," I said.

"Pretty classy, eh?" she said. "Shows off my boobs. I've still got great boobs."

"Congratulations, Mom," I said. I didn't want to think about her boobs.

"No, Charlie," she said, with surprising mildness: "You're not going to ruin my good mood. I've got great boobs. Oh, and I'm going for a manicure."

"Yeah?" I said.

"And a pedicure."

"Great," I said. This wasn't something you did on a social assistance cheque.

"Your friends will be coming by in a little bit," she said, suddenly remembering.

"Which friends?" I said—but I knew.

"The rich ones," said Barb. "They were out for a walk and they stopped in to see you. They said they'd try you again on the way back." She was still primping.

"Did you thank them for the dress?" I asked.

"Of course I thanked them for the dress," said Barb, meeting my eyes in the mirror. "Do you think I'm a goddamn ingrate?"

"No, Mom," I said. But I was feeling very wary about the arrangement that seemed to have been made between my mother and the Boormans. "Do you know where they were walking?"

"They were going for ice cream." She adjusted the front of her dress, and bent over a little to judge the effect on her bust.

"Okay. I'll go meet them," I said.

"D'you want some money for a cone?" Barb asked casually.

"Do you have money for ice cream?" I said incredulously.

"Of course I have," said Barb. "I've always been a good money manager. Here." And she hauled a buck out of her purse.

"Thanks," I said. But I did not feel grateful so much as heavy-hearted. My mother had clearly been bought.

"But that's all you're getting," she said, reverting to type as she took a new tube of lipstick from her handbag and began to apply it, baring her teeth in the process. I watched her for a moment or two, then slipped back out.

If I'm fair—and I want to be fair—I need to tell one other story about Barb that puts her in a slightly different light. On my sixteenth birthday, about a year and a bit before that summer, my mother proposed an early evening walk. I was surprised, but I agreed, and so it happened that we found ourselves, eventually, on the main street of Greenfield, somewhere between the funeral home and the beer store. We hadn't been talking much, but we hadn't been silent either. We'd lived in the village long enough that we knew, between us, a fair number of people, so we'd spoken, a little, about the family who ran the hardware, and about Doug the barber, and about the ladies in the bulk food place, as we passed by their various storefronts. Barb told me she thought Doug was getting rich off real estate investments, and that someone had sprinkled dried marijuana leaves into the herbal tea bin at the bulk food place back in 1968, and the ladies had been distraught for weeks afterwards. We laughed about that—and we hardly ever laughed together.

Barb was between boyfriends at that point, and she'd been drinking a fair bit for a few weeks. She'd stayed off the booze throughout this particular day, however, and she was lucid, even sharp, on our walk. She was as close to being her real self, then, as it was possible for her to be.

We were walking along, talking a little, when we glimpsed, coming towards us, two women in their early forties. Their hair styles and bearing made it clear that they were from a higher social bracket than we were, and they were obviously walking for exercise: they were even wearing work-out clothes and fancy running shoes. When Barb saw them, she stiffened up—though she kept walking. She looked wary and defensive.

As the two of us came close to the two of them, I saw the women's faces assume expressions of disdain—even contempt. But they weren't looking at me, the awkward teenage boy; they were looking at Barb. I stepped to one side to let them pass, and it took me a moment or two to catch up with my mother, who never slackened her pace. When I did catch up, I looked at her, intending to say something, but her jaw was set and there were tears in her eyes, so I thought better of it. From behind me, I heard one of the women we'd passed laughing about something. The word *slut* floated back towards us.

Barb said nothing. I said nothing. We made our way home, and Barb began to drink.

That very same year, the year I turned sixteen, I was home on the evening of December 22nd or 23rd, when I heard a scuffling outside our front door. I had been wrapping my mom's Christmas present—a pack of Virginia Slims and a coffee mug—at the kitchen table, so I went over to the kitchen window to look out. I arrived just in time to see two teenage girls disappear around the side of the house: it looked as though they were running. Something about the hair of one of them was vaguely familiar, but she was wearing a long winter coat so I couldn't identify her for sure. I thought, though, that it might be Tammy from my class at school—or maybe Gail.

Not knowing what else to do, I went to the front door and opened it, not really expecting anything, but thinking I should see if there was any sign of why they'd come. On our front step was a basket covered with cellophane and a big red bow. I didn't at first realize that it was a Christmas hamper. I'd never seen one before.

But that's what it was. I hauled it inside, and I took off the cellophane, and there, nestled in fake straw, was a sealed envelope, a tin of oysters, a large can of Ye Olde English plum pudding, a tin of peas, two Christmas crackers, four mandarin oranges, a package of shelled walnuts, and a small frozen turkey. I was astonished. My astonishment deepened when I opened the envelope to find a Christmas card picturing a star over a stable. Inside the card said, simply, "Happy Christmas, Mrs. Knowles and Charlie!" It was not signed.

When Barb came home, she was livid. "Do they think I'm a fucking charity case?" she raged. Nevertheless, she roasted the turkey on Christmas day, and we ate it, though she wouldn't touch the oysters or the plum pudding.

I'd almost forgotten about the hamper when I returned to school in January, but I was sitting in the cafeteria playing euchre when I glanced up to see two girls looking at me intently—and I recognized the hair of the taller of the two: it was Tammy. They both smiled at me—but I found myself suddenly consumed by embarrassment and shame. I ducked my head, then tried to give every calorie of my energy to the card game. I'm pretty sure the girl I recognized was the daughter of one of the women Barb and I had passed on our walk. And I was her charity project.

Serge had taken me to the Dairy Queen a few days before he and Selina came by my house. A young woman had served him, and he had flirted with her, subtly but to devastating effect. She had blushed and beamed and all but melted when he ordered two vanilla cones and a smile to go. I knew her from school—she had been in my geography class—but I might as well have been invisible for all the attention she gave me.

Half a block from the DQ I could see Selina on the patio, her blonde hair radiant in the late afternoon sun. She was talking with a young mother and her small daughter, and the child was showing her something: Selina bent to look at it closely, then laughed and put a hand on the little girl's head as she straightened up. She and the mother laughed together, too, as they parted, and in the same instant Serge came outside with an ice cream cone and leaving, I was sure, at least one fluttering teenage heart in his wake. Selina took the cone from Serge, then took his arm, and they stepped off the patio and headed towards me. Turning from her husband to look ahead of her, Selina saw me for the first time and waved enthusiastically. "Yoo hoo, Charlie!" she called.

"Hi," I called back, and gave a half-wave. In truth, at least a part of my heart thrilled to see her, to see both of them, but it wasn't in the culture of teenage males at that time and in that place to show raw enthusiasm—not in public. But Selina's smile did not fade.

"Can we take you back for an ice cream cone, Charlie?" asked Serge as we drew nearer.

"Thanks, but I have my own money," I said. "I'll get one later."

We came together, and Selina disengaged herself from Serge, giving him her cone to hold, and held out both her hands to me. "I'm so excited your mother will let you come with us!" she said.

I hesitated fractionally, but then took both of her hands. "Yeah, it's good news," I said.

"And she looks so lovely in her dress!" said Selina.

"She looks great," I said. "Thanks, again. I think it really ... softened her up."

"Well, well," said Serge. "There's nothing like helping bring out a woman's natural beauty to make her happy. My Selina is sunny all the time!"

"Because you buy me such nice presents, you mean?" said Selina playfully.

"No," said Serge. "Because you are so naturally beautiful."

"He's so sweet to me," said Selina to me. Then: "Oh, look, Serge! Look! Do you see that mock orange? I must have a closer look. I'll be back!"

"Take your cone!" said Serge laughing—and she took it before almost running down the sidewalk and into the front yard of a house just down the street. Not for the first time, Serge and I watched her in appreciative silence.

"She's a fine woman, my wife," said Serge. "I've been lucky in love, Charlie. Very lucky." I was silent. For some reason—and I don't why—for some reason I was suddenly overwhelmed by a sense of my own smallness and insignificance. It was as if I were projected outside of myself, and then made to turn and look back at the shell I'd left behind. And what did I see? I saw a plain-looking boy of seventeen in a pair of faded jeans and a T-shirt that needed a wash—still a year away from graduating from a low-rent, warehouse-like high school in rural Ontario. He read, spoke and understood only a single language. He had no money in the bank. He could find no work other than occasional grass-cutting. His mother was a welfare queen. And the previous evening he'd begun—stopped, yes, but *begun*—to rape a small, fragile, defenceless foreign girl. I was, I saw, about as low and contemptible as a human being could get. I could feel the bile of self-disgust rise in my throat.

"Is something wrong?" asked Serge. "You're rather subdued, Charlie."

"What's your interest in me?" I burst out. "I'm just a snot-nosed kid next to you and Selina. I've never been anywhere, I've never done anything. I don't *know* anything." There were tears in my eyes.

"Charlie, Charlie, Charlie," said Serge. "What is this?" His face was a study of concern—his eyes at once sympathetic and genuinely puzzled. He leaned towards me a little.

"I want to know why you and Selina became my friends," I said, and I heard my mother's voice asserting itself in my own tones.

"Why not?" said Serge. "You're a charming young man." His eyes were directly on mine, and they seemed so sincere, so filled with kindness, that it was difficult not to trust him.

"I'm not," I said. "I'm ... nothing. I'm *shit*—that's what I am. I'm all confused."

Serge looked at me carefully, gently before replying. "Charlie," he said, "you're underestimating yourself. You're a good person, Charlie. You're a good person, and you were looking for love. We—Selina and I—were more than happy to share ours."

And there it was: a beautiful, humane, loving answer. Wasn't it? *Wasn't it*? Or was it? What made me challenge it? Was it my own smallness of spirit—my moral wretchedness—or was it a small spark of decency in me—a spark that Milly had fanned into life—that recognized that the darkest souls can tell the lightest lies? "I saw what you did," I said.

"What I did," said Serge, clearly puzzled.

"To Milly. I saw."

"What we did to Milly," said Serge. "When was this?" (Did he really not know? Or was he so cool, so polished, that he could pretend to have no idea what I was talking about?)

"At the picnic," I said. "In the woods."

"Ah," said Serge, apparently understanding at last. "Well." He shrugged. "Sometimes a man likes to have another woman. And my wife, as you saw, doesn't mind. Selina takes pleasure in my pleasure. But I'm sad to hear you were spying on us, Charlie. That is strange behaviour from a friend."

"You're changing the subject," I said.

"Am I?" said Serge.

"Yes!" I said. "You're trying to make me feel bad for what I saw, but it's you who did the awful thing."

Serge took out his silver cigarette case, but his eyes never left mine as he opened it and took out a cigarette. "I will say this gently, Charlie," he said. "Selina and I saved Milly's life. We gave her a home, and we helped her to heal. When she recovered, we gave her a job. When you consider what she is and what we did for her, I think we have a right to expect a little recreation from her. And the thing you don't know, the thing you can't be expected to understand, is that you were seeing a kind of game. It's a very adult game, yes, and easy to misinterpret or misunderstand if you see only a piece of it, but it's a game that gives Milly pleasure, too." He smiled after he said this—the smile of a worldly adult male—and I wanted to believe him. I almost did.

"It didn't look like a game," I said.

"It is, as I say, a very adult game," said Serge, and he lit his cigarette. "You are a bright and charming young man, Charlie, but you are not yet fully grown. One day you will understand." He exhaled, and looked at me without expression.

"You're right," I said. "I don't understand."

"Life is complex," said Serge. "*Ambiguous*. I wonder if Mr. Boone has taught you that word, Charlie? Not everything is clear to us. But haven't you taken pleasure in Selina's company and my own? Have we not been good to you?"

"I don't know," I said, and I began to back away from him. I needed to be somewhere else. I needed to be somewhere I could think things through without his warm, manly, reasonable voice filling my head and rearranging the mental furniture.

"Charlie..." said Serge, and he held out a hand to me.

"I don't know what to think!" I cried.

"Come," said Serge. "There's no need for us to dwell on this. Let's—"

"I don't know what's true," I erupted. "I don't know what's right! I need to go—" and I turned and ran.

I looked back just once. Selina had returned to Serge and he was speaking to her. I can guess at their conversation, but guessing is all I can do.

The day had already been filled with walks, and the walking was not over. I wandered for the next three hours anyway, until dusk began to threaten. I wandered the streets of Greenfield, and I wandered through the fields, and I went down by the river, too; and everywhere I went I tried to see my way clear, to push past my profound confusion. Was it possible that Milly *had* been playing a kind of game? No: much as I mistrusted myself on so many fronts, I was confident I had seen trauma on her face and heard it in her voice. But if Serge and Selina were wicked, *reptilian*, how was I to account for their treatment of me? Could people be both good and evil, righteous and repellent? Had they been warm and generous with me even while they were doing everything needed to destroy Milly? Could they love me—*love*!—at the same time that they denied Milly's very humanity?

Or was there something even more sinister going on? Had they been *grooming* me, in some way, to take Milly's place? Had they once treated Milly with the same apparent consideration and kindness they had shown me? I didn't know the answers then.

Mr. Boone lived in one of the newer neighbourhoods to the west of the village: it wasn't as nice a street as Hazelwood, but it was a good deal nicer than my own. The houses were relatively new, but some of them had been built with old-fashioned porches, and Mr. Boone was sitting on his screened front porch reading a newspaper and drinking an iced tea when I found my way to his home. I suspect I looked a little distraught.

"Hello, Charlie," said Mr. Boone, rising and opening the screen door. "Did you just fall from the sky?" He looked at me with some concern, both eyebrows raised and his head tilted.

"No, sir," I said. "I was just walking by."

"You were just walking by," said Mr. Boone. "Well, have a seat and tell me what's on your mind. Would you like a drink?"

"No, thank you, sir," I said.

"It's iced tea," said Mr. Boone. "I make a mean glass of iced tea."

I hesitated. "Sure," I said. "That would be nice."

"Have a seat, Charlie," said Mr. Boone. "I'll be back in a moment."

I sat down and Mr. Boone went inside. I heard him a moment later saying something to someone—probably his wife. Both their voices were gentle, subdued. Somewhere in the house a radio was tuned to the CBC. Mr. Boone had laid his newspaper aside, but next to his chair there was a stack of books: something about the Renaissance, a novel by Robertson Davies, and a bird-watching handbook. The porch smelled vaguely of home cooking and pine cleanser, and the street was a quiet one. I felt as though I'd stumbled into a kind of oasis.

Mr. Boone returned and handed me a tall glass of iced tea: he'd put a slice of lemon on the rim. "If it needs a little more sugar just say the word," he said.

"Thank you, sir," I said. "I'm sure it's just right."

Mr. Boone sat down again. "Well, Charlie," he said, "is this just a social visit? Or do you have something on your mind?"

"I have something on my mind, sir," I said. "A question."

"A question?" said Mr. Boone. He was looking at me as closely as Serge had. "Well, fire away whenever you're ready."

I took a deep draught of my tea, then put the glass down on the small table beside me. Stealing a look at Mr. Boone revealed he was no longer gazing at me: instead his face was inclined downward, his eyes closed. I sensed he was waiting—not wanting to push. My question came out in a rush: "What would you do if you knew something bad was going on and you wanted it to stop, but that badness was in you, too?"

Mr. Boone was silent for a moment. Then he said, "This isn't just an academic question, is it, Charlie?"

"What do you mean?" I asked.

"I mean, you didn't come over here to ask me this question out of idle curiosity. The answer matters, doesn't it?" He looked at me over his glass of tea.

"Yes, sir," I said.

"Do you want to tell me what it's about?"

"No. No, I don't," I said. I *did* want to tell him—at least part of it—but I couldn't bear to have him know the full truth. I wanted him to like me still.

"All right," said Mr. Boone. He thought for a moment. "Let me see if I've got it, then. You know of something wrong that's going on that you think should be stopped, but you're not sure what to do because you recognize that you're not perfect either?"

"The same kind of wrong is in me," I said. The words had tumbled out of me, and I wondered if I'd said too much.

"The same kind of wrong is in you," repeated Mr. Boone. He took a spoon he'd left on his own small table and slowly stirred the ice in his drink. He was really thinking, I saw: he wasn't trying to rush me off with a half-baked answer. After a moment or two he seemed to come to a conclusion. "All right. Charlie," he said, laying the spoon aside: "we're none of us perfect: there's good stuff and bad stuff in all of us. Okay?"

I nodded.

"We're none of us angels, Charlie. We're all flesh and blood."

"Yes, sir," I said.

"If you have a chance to stop something that's wrong, I don't think you should hesitate just because you've done wrong, too." He looked at me for the first time in a little while. His eyes were absolutely focused on me.

"Okay," I said.

"That's what I think, at least," he said. "Does that help at all?"

"Yes, sir," I said. "It really does." I drained my glass, stood up, and looked directly at my former teacher. "Thank you, sir," I said.

"You don't have to go right away, Charlie," said Mr. Boone.

"Thank you, sir," I said again, "But I have to think about what I'm going to do."

Mr. Boone raised his glass to me, and I suspect he watched me out of sight.

So I went back home, and I went into the kitchen, and I sat down at the table and put my head in my hands. In some part of my mind I knew that I should eat and drink, but I felt neither hunger nor thirst. Barb came downstairs from her room and stood in the doorway.

"Like my nails?" she said.

I wasn't sure I'd heard her right. "What?" I said.

"Like my nails?" she repeated. "I've had a manicure." She held them up for my inspection. They'd clearly had some expert attention, and for the first time in my memory their colour was appealing rather than garish.

"They're fine, Mom," I said.

"Look at them!" said Barb. "You're not looking at them." She splayed her hands out in front of me. That close her fingernails looked like talons—but they were, in any event, well-groomed talons.

I looked at them. "They're fine," I said. "They look good."

"I've always liked nice things," said Barb. "That's the problem with having kids. You have to sacrifice so much." She reached into her handbag and pulled out a pack of cigarettes. "How were your friends?"

"Fine," I said.

"I still don't trust them, you know," said Barb.

"No?" I said. I looked into her face.

"No. I think something's funny about them," said Barb, and her face took on a curiously twisted appearance—a sort of Randyish cast. "I don't think they're really married," she said. "Have they ever shown you their wedding pictures?"

"No," I said.

"If they were married, they'd have shown you their wedding pictures," said Barb. "I think they're just living together."

I stared at my mother.

"What's the matter?" asked Barb. For a moment she seemed genuinely interested in my welfare, and for a moment I considered trusting her and telling her what I had seen and done. The moment passed, however: there was too much bad history between us.

"Nothing," I said dully.

"I'm gonna show Roger my nails. And my dress."

"Okay," I said.

"I may stay over there tonight."

"Fine," I said.

Barb nodded, then disappeared. She reappeared a moment later, however. "Charlie," she said.

"What?"

"Don't fuck it up with these people," she said.

"What do you mean?" I asked.

"I mean we can do okay out of this," she said. "Do you understand me?"

"Yup," I said.

"So don't fuck it up," she repeated. She fixed me with her eyes, and I felt a weight descend upon my heart. I was going to have to do something that would be very hard to do. And I would have to do it soon. "There's some canned soup above the stove," she said.

She left again, but this time I heard the front door open and close. I thought for a moment, and saw that I had no choice other than to fuck it up: I owed that much to Milly. I picked up the phone and dialled. "Serge?" I said. "It's Charlie. Listen to me. There's something you need to do. You need to do the right thing by Milly. You need to set her free, and give her the money she needs to be okay. Because if you don't..."

I'd feared I wouldn't find the words—but I found them. Serge was quiet, but very angry.

Ten

I mowed lawns the next day. All day. I just went up and down the streets of Mr. Boone's neighbourhood knocking on doors and offering my services. At first most people politely refused me, but I quickly learned to open with my price: it was very cheap. I went home at the end of the day exhausted, and confident I would sleep late into the next morning—but my eyes opened at 5:00 a.m. and I could not go back to sleep. I went walking, then, across the fields, into the woods, and eventually down to the river. It was there, as I was walking alone, that I stumbled upon Milly. She was standing on the bank staring out into the water. "Hi," she said.

"Hi," I replied. I felt sure she would want to be alone. "I'll go away. I had no idea you were here."

"No. It is all right," she said. She was wearing her modest blue dress, but she'd also put on a baseball cap.

"I'm sorry—" I said.

"Please. It is all right. You stopped." Her voice was clear and firm.

"Thank you," I said. And I meant it in more ways than I can easily convey.

There was a brief pause. Milly looked out at the water again. "I am leaving," she said, at length.

"You're leaving the Boormans?" I asked.

"Yes."

"Do they know?" I asked. But I knew they knew. I wondered what Milly would do. Would she go back to school? Would she try to find another job in domestic service?

"Mr. Boorman gave me some money," said Milly. "He said I should go."

"And you're pleased?" I hoped desperately she was.

"I am free," she said simply—and she turned to me and smiled.

"Do you have somewhere to go?" I asked.

"I will find somewhere," Milly said. And then: "Do you believe in God, Mr. Charlie?"

"I don't know," I said, a little startled. "It's not something I've really thought about. Why?"

She was quiet for a moment, then she stooped to pick up a rock. She held it in her hand and stared at it. "When I first came to Canada," she said, "I worked for some very strange people. They were not gentle with each other. They were not gentle with their children. I became sick because I could not deal with all the anger."

"You had a nervous breakdown," I said, remembering what she'd told me.

"Yes," she said. "I had a nervous breakdown. And while I was sick, I prayed and prayed and prayed that God would deliver me. Do you understand? I prayed that God would set me free from these people, and help me to find a job with a family that did not yell and hit each other."

I nodded. "Yes, I understand."

"One day," said Milly, "I was sitting in a park watching the children, and I was crying, and this lovely lady sat down next to me, and she took my hand in hers, and asked me what was wrong."

"Selina," I said. I could see it as if I were watching a film.

"Yes. Selina. And two days later I was sleeping in one of their bedrooms, and there were flowers on the chest of drawers, and Selina brought me meals on a tray. And it seemed that God had answered my prayers." The sun glinted off the water. Somewhere a little downstream a fish leapt above the surface of the water. I kept my eyes on Milly's face. There was no emotion on the surface, but I suspected that her feelings ran very deep. "And then things changed," she said.

There was a silence between us: at that instant, I didn't know what to say. Milly suddenly cocked her arm and threw her rock into the river. "Sometimes God seems to want us to work things out for ourselves," she said. There was no bitterness in her voice.

I thought about that for a moment. And I've thought about it a lot in the years since. "I think I know what you mean," I said.

"Do you?" she said. "I think you do."

I picked up a rock myself, and sent it skipping over the water's surface—once, twice, thrice. I was about to bend and pick up another, but Milly touched my arm and pointed: a small flock of Canada geese was approaching our stretch of the river, low and fast. A moment later and they landed, honking furiously, and began to swim upstream. We watched them. I felt no urge to do them harm. "They're free, too," I said. I wondered what had been behind my anger the last time I saw them.

"Good-bye, Mr. Charlie," said Milly. I turned to her. She looked at me for a moment, smiled gravely, and left. I looked down at the ground, worried—absurdly, I think—that even a lingering gaze might be a species of profanation. But the ache I felt was a good ache.

The rest of the summer was not without incident, but what incident it had bears little relation to this story. I worked more and more as the summer unfolded: I built up quite a clientele for my lawn-cutting, and I branched out a little into setting sprinklers when people were away on holiday, and putting out their garbage. I saw Serge and Selina twice that August, both times at a distance. Late in the month Roger told Barb that the Boormans' house was up for sale, and I think it sold fairly quickly. Barb was bitterly disappointed, but she'd lost so much already that she swiftly put this most recent disappointment into a place with all the others. To my surprise, she didn't blame me—or at least, not much: I don't think she imagined that I might have any agency when it came to influencing the rich and generous. It was as though my projected trip to Europe had been an idle fantasy, though it left at least a few traces: her red dress, some expensive perfume, an elegant pair of high-heeled shoes.

In the next year I finished my high school at Champlain, and with Mr. Boone's encouragement, and the help of a guidance counsellor, I made out three university applications. All three schools accepted me, and one even offered a scholarship. I accepted it. So it was that one morning in early September of 1976 I found myself at the Voyageur bus terminal stowing a battered suitcase below the coach. "Ticket, son?" said the driver, and I passed it over. He tore off half, and returned the other half to me. I climbed on board the coach.

Barb was standing by the terminal. She was staring at the coach, her face a mixture of resentment ... and something else. Was it sorrow? Perhaps it was envy. I'm not sure. She was not there to bless me, but she was there. She was wearing a pair of jeans and an old plaid shirt of Roger's. I wore a Queen's T-shirt courtesy of the alum who was funding my scholarship.

I took my seat, looked out at my mother, and raised my hand in a kind of salute. She did not return it, but then maybe she didn't see me through the tinted windows. I looked away from the window, and closed my eyes.

I haven't been back.

Two strange things befell me during my years at Queen's University.

In my first year, I briefly went out with a lovely young woman called Julia. She was small and slight and bright and green-eyed and gorgeous. She spoke with a lisp that I found enchanting. The relationship didn't last longer than a few months: I fell deeply in love, but she wasn't ready for the kind of commitment I so desperately wanted. She ended things as gently as she could, but I still bled emotionally for weeks afterwards.

Before we parted company, though—before I drove her off—we visited her parents and sister at Thanksgiving, and this was my first sustained exposure to a happy family. We sat down to a Thanksgiving dinner that Julia's mother had spent hours preparing, and Julia's dad said grace: and when he said grace he said a special thank you for the work his wife had done in cooking the meal. And during dinner we talked about what Julia and I were learning at university, and about her younger sister's drama class at high school, and about books and music and a family friend of theirs who had recently opened a new business. We talked about sad things, too, but mostly the topics were light and they—we—laughed. We laughed just as much as I had laughed in the brief good times with Serge and Selina.

After dinner, Julia and I washed the dishes and cleaned up, and then we went for a walk in the neighbourhood. It was a leafy suburb, and the residents were clearly proud of their homes and well-disposed to their neighbours. We were greeted by several people on our walk: we had to stop and chat and Julia introduced me and told whoever had stopped us what her life was like at Queen's. I wanted to find somewhere quiet and private to make out, but it didn't happen.

Later that evening, after Julia's mother and sister had gone to bed, Julia and I sat in the living room and talked; her dad was still up and he made tea for the three of us. At some point, the phone rang; it was Julia's grandmother calling from Ireland to see how she was, so she was gone for some minutes. This, of course, left her dad, James, and me alone.

James was a pipe-smoker. After Julia had gone off to the kitchen to take the call he took some time to prepare and light his pipe: it was clearly a little ritual. He even involved me, to the extent that he asked me to open the windows behind him. When the pipe was lit, and burning to his satisfaction, he puffed on it for a moment or two, then fixed me with eyes that were disconcertingly like his daughter's.

"I think you're quite fond of Julia," he said.

"Yes, sir," I replied. "I'm in love with her."

"Well, that's nice," said James reflectively, and he drew on his pipe, regarding me all the while. He didn't say anything else.

"I'm hoping we'll get married," I said, desperate to fill the silence. "If she'll have me, I mean," I added.

"Yes," said James. "Well, there is that." He looked thoughtfully into the bowl of his pipe.

"Maybe we'll have to finish school first," I gabbled on. "The whole four years. I don't mean next summer."

"Yes," he said. "Well, you don't want to rush into things." Then he fixed me again with his eyes. "I think you are a good person, Charlie."

"Thank you, sir," I said—but I was stunned that he'd used precisely the same words Serge had used just a year and a bit before.

"I think you are a good person," he repeated, "but I think you should be patient about finding love. It will come. If you were my son, I would counsel you to be a good friend before you try to be something more." He picked up his mug of tea with his free hand and took a sip.

"Yes, sir," I said.

"Good friends are important," he said. "And friendship can be a rehearsal for marriage."

"Yes, sir," I said again. I was beginning to realize that this was not a casual conversation.

"You and Julia are very young. It's good that you're friends. But it would be wrong to rush into intimacy."

"Yes, sir," I said, "but—"

"I'm glad we understand each other," he said, and he drew on his pipe again. The conversation was clearly over. And whenever I tried to make out with Julia after that, his image arose spontaneously in my mind. Indeed, so vivid was that image, that I swore I could even smell his pipe tobacco. It was a powerful anti-aphrodisiac.

But what stayed with me most powerfully was the recognition

that James and Serge and Mr. Boone all had a great deal in common. They were all very clever men, in their different ways; they all listened well; they all commanded respect. And it struck me that on first acquaintance, and even for some time afterwards, it would be impossible to know which of them was deeply flawed—which of the three would use his gifts to do something hideous. And that thought had a corollary: if *one* of them could, might not *all* of them? In the right circumstances, might my old teacher and my girlfriend's father be as cold and ruthless as Serge? I don't think so—I really don't—but I cannot be sure. And that made me wonder if I too could, if I wished, conceal a malign intent; and I saw that I would have to make a choice, every day, as to what kind of man I wished to be; that the fear of being caught and punished would never be sufficient to make me good.

In my third year at Queen's, in the spring term, I woke up around two in the morning in a cold sweat. I don't know what I'd been dreaming, but I was thinking intensely about Randy. And I doubt I'd thought about Randy in any serious way since I left Greenfield. He hadn't come back to do a fifth year at Champlain, so I hadn't had so much as a fleeting conversation with him in years. I was able to get back to sleep eventually, and I did not knowingly dream again that night, but later that morning I told my then girlfriend, Peggy, what had happened.

In the afternoon of that day I ran into one of the few other people from Champlain who had come to Queen's since my own high school graduation. Pete Howe, a soccer-playing commerce major, told me he'd had a call earlier in the day from his younger sister back home, and she'd told him that Randy had killed himself a few hours before. He'd slit his wrists in the bath like some ancient Roman.

That was shocking enough—shocking on all kinds of levels—but the kicker for me came about a week later when an envelope arrived from Greenfield addressed simply to

Charlie Knowles
Queen's University
Kingston, Ontario
(He's a student there)

I marvelled that Canada Post had discovered me, but the joke that was forming on my lips died when I realized that the envelope had been sent by Randy, and must have been mailed the day before he killed himself. There was no letter, but there was a grotesque pencil sketch of a young woman who looked vaguely like Milly, and Randy—for it seemed that Randy had drawn the picture—had scrawled two words across the bottom. "Worth it?" It was a weird, deranged thing to do.

Weird and deranged. But perhaps it wasn't just Randy. Perhaps it was the zeitgeist. Six people from Greenfield killed themselves that spring and early summer. Six people in their late teens or early twenties. It was as though a small hell gate had opened underneath the village. There was a community meeting about it, and the province sent in social workers and psychologists, and it made the national news. But I'd already moved on. It's not that I didn't care; I just didn't want to be *from* there any longer. I didn't want Greenfield to be part of the definition of who I was and who I might become.

A year after I graduated Queen's, I was living in Toronto and working at a small advertising agency. It was a stepping-stone job, an interim sort of thing. I was in a bar, waiting for a friend to arrive, when I saw an attractive woman dancing wildly all by herself. Her hair was a different colour, and her dress was provocatively short, but I instantly recognized Selina.

When the song ended, Selina collected herself and moved to the bar. I stared at her for a moment longer, then gathered my courage and went up to her. "Selina?" I said.

Selina didn't look in the least surprised to see me—and maybe she *had* seen me before I saw her. "Hello, Charlie," she said, and she lit a cigarette. Up close I could see that she was wearing more makeup than she had in her Greenfield days: her lipstick had been applied with a heavy hand, and there was some sort of glitter on her cheeks. Her breasts looked bigger than I remembered, though the effect could have been produced with a push-up bra and a dress that revealed more than it hid.

"Are you alone?" I asked.

"As you see," she said, exhaling.

"May I buy you a drink?" I wasn't sure what else to say, and I was certainly curious about her.

"I have one," she said. And she tinkled the ice in her glass.

"Where is Serge?" I asked, looking around.

"Serge and I are no longer together," she said and, seeing the blank look on my face: "That surprises you?"

"Yes. Yes, it does," I said.

"Welcome to the world," she said, and laughed. It was a harsh laugh—quite unlike the girlish laugh I remembered. "So what are you doing?" she said.

"I'm sort of interning with an advertising agency—" I began, but Selina cut me off.

"No," she said. "What are you doing *tonight*?" She leaned forward a little, and I found I didn't like her perfume: its muskiness reminded me uncomfortably of Barb's. And remembering Barb's perfume made me think of Barb herself, living much the same life she always had back in Greenfield, though the boyfriends were, I gathered, a little harder to find.

"Oh. Nothing," I said. "I'm just here for a drink. And to listen to the music. I come here sometimes."

"Would you like to fuck me?" she asked.

I was stunned. I stared at her. "I don't know what to say," I said.

"Try yes." She was looking at my mouth, as if trying to assess what pleasure my tongue might give her. Or perhaps she didn't want to look into my eyes.

"Well, I'm honoured," I said, "but—"

"Are you here with a girl?"

"No, I'm meeting—"

"Are you gay?" She cocked her head at me.

"No! No, it's not that—" I said.

"Do you find me too old?" asked Selina. She put a hand on my knee, and my body responded involuntarily to hers. She was still sexy. I was young. I recalled vividly what I'd done to her, and she to me, in a hundred fantasies.

"No," I said. "I find you very attractive."

"So what's the problem?" she said.

I paused. What was the problem? After all, why not just fuck her? Why the hell not? "I don't know who you are," I said, the words tumbling out of my mouth without me summoning them.

"Is that important?" she said.

"Yes," I said.

"I'm the best lay you'll ever have," she said, and for just an instant her tongue licked her lower lip.

"That's not what I mean," I said.

"Then what do you mean, Charlie?" Direct. Pointed.

"I'm very conventional, Selina," I said. "I need to know the person I'm with. I need to be able to *trust* who she is." And in saying this, I discovered that I believed it. I had learned it from her, in a way, by way of Milly, and it felt oddly satisfying to give it back to her.

Selina stubbed out her cigarette, and rose to leave. "Good night, then," she said.

"Good night, Mrs. Boorman," I replied.

"Fuck off," she said. Her voice was ice-cold. She took a few steps away, then turned and looked me in the eyes. "Oh, do you remember Milly?" she said. "I think you were fond of her."

"I remember Milly," I said.

"She's dead," Selina said. "A car accident. Such a shame."

"Oh my god," I said—genuinely shocked.

Selina shrugged, turned and left. I felt sick and desperately sad. Which, of course, was the point.

ELEVEN

Two years later, I was twenty-five, still living in downtown Toronto and working in corporate communications for one of the major Canadian banks. Mostly it involved writing profiles of bank executives for the in-house newsletter. It was dull work, then, but it allowed me to rent a nice apartment and go out a couple of nights a week. It also allowed me to send Barb a little cheque every month—enough to pay the phone bill, with a bit left over for a beer or two. She never wrote me, but she always cashed the cheque.

The best part of my job was that it exposed me to a great gaggle of single young women in the secretarial and junior executive pool, so I dated quite a bit. And if my teenage years had been marked by relatively few opportunities for sexual intimacy, I made up for it then. I was a reasonably presentable young man with a decent degree from a good school, and my village roots were well hidden. So I played the field. But I was looking for more—still looking for love. Real love. And I hadn't yet found it.

On a warm Friday in July I met up with Helen, a girl I'd met through work, and took her out to dinner at an Indian restaurant, Spices, near Toronto General Hospital. The meal was first class: mulligatawny soup, samosas, chicken korma, and a delicately flavoured rice pudding to end with. We drank Kingfisher beer with the main course, and chased the rice pudding with chai. And we talked, both of us, not compulsively, but with a growing sense that there was much to exchange, much to share. She told me about the breakdown of her parents' marriage when she was in her early teens, and the final, angst-filled year during which she was sent away to a private school in Switzerland. I talked mostly about my time at Queen's, though I did mention that I'd grown up, the only child of a single mother, in Greenfield. It turned out that Helen's family used to have a cottage on Rocky Lake, about twenty minutes from my old home.

And then, after dinner, out into the mildly humid evening, the warmth of the day still remembered in the sidewalks. We strolled along Gerrard for a while, then headed south, deciding it might be fun to hear some jazz. When we hit Queen Street West, Helen took my arm, her own slipping under my elbow, and I felt, suddenly, almost weightless, as if her touch magically lifted the weight of a deep loneliness from my shoulders.

We eventually found a small jazz bar and went inside, seated at our table by a friendly but harried Jamaican waitress. She lit a candle in a small glass bowl and set it between us, then bustled off with our drink orders. I reached out and took Helen's hand across the table. She wore a sparkling blue gem in a thin band of gold.

"What is it?" I asked.

"A sapphire," she said. "It was a gift."

"I don't know anything about gems," I said. "Poetry I know something about, but I can't tell a diamond from a moonstone."

"Bet you could," she said, smiling at me. And she did not withdraw her hand.

Jazz had been playing on a sound system when we came in, but now a rather chubby man in his early thirties shuffled out of a back room, turned the music off, sat down at the piano, nodded at the six or seven occupied tables, rested his fingers on the keys for a moment, then began to play. I didn't recognize the tune, and realized after a couple of minutes that the pianist was improvising, taking a theme and playing with it—pushing its edges, turning it over, bending it out of shape, and then, miraculously, rediscovering its form in the chaos he'd conjured around it. It was far better playing than I'd expected to hear, and I was pleased to see that Helen was as impressed and caught up in the music as I was.

We applauded warmly when the piece was over, and the pianist turned and smiled at us, his chubby form imbued now with a power that flowed from his fingertips up. "Any requests?"

I looked at Helen. "As Time Goes By"? she said, making the request a question. "But I'm happy if you just keep doing what you're doing."

"As Time Goes By," said the pianist, and he turned back to the piano, paused a moment, then launched into an extended exploration of the tune, discovering in its simple structure a world of subtlety and nuance. It was a virtuoso performance. Conversation would have been a minor blasphemy.

When the set was done, and the pianist shuffled back to the back room, I caught the waitress's eye and she came to our table. "What's the name of the pianist?" I asked.

"Stephan," she replied.

"Please give Stephan a glass of wine from us—or a beer, if that's what he drinks."

"He drinks Spanish coffee," she said.

"That's fine," I said. She nodded, and left.

"That was amazing," said Helen. "He's really talented."

"He is," I said. "And he's a young guy to be playing with that kind of authority."

We had returned, for a few minutes, to talking about Helen's family, when the pianist made his way over to our table, holding his Spanish coffee. He sat down at the unoccupied table next to ours, but then moved his seat over towards us.

"Thank you for the drink," he said. He was wearing an extra-large black dress shirt tucked into a pair of chinos. While he was, as I mentioned, a bit on the heavy side, there was a certain grace to his movement.

"You're welcome," I said.

"Thank you for the beautiful playing," said Helen.

"It is my gift," said Stephan, putting down his drink and raising his hands to the level of his face, his fingers spread. "My fingers know things that my brain does not." His accent was difficult to place. East European, perhaps. Polish? Hungarian? I could not be sure. My attention was drawn to Stephan's hands: they were smaller than I would have expected, and the fingers were a little stubby. They didn't look like the hands of a brilliant pianist.

We learned that Stephan was a mixture of Serb and Croat, and that he had lived for some years in Manchester before deciding to follow his brothers out to Canada. And he told us he made his living by playing there, in the jazz bar, five nights a week, and by teaching piano. He was happy to answer our questions until, eventually, we ran out of them. I was beginning to wish, mildly, that he'd resume playing, and leave me alone to hold Helen's hand.

"I will show you something," said Stephan suddenly. He gestured to the waitress, and she moved forward as though she'd been expecting his summons. She carried with her a large pottery vase, in the bottom of which there were a couple of hundred Skittles—little fruit-flavoured candies of uniform shape and size, but each bearing one of six different colours. They were all mixed up in the bowl.

"Sweets," said Stephan. "Skittles. Like Smarties, maybe, but no chocolate. You see the different colours?"

"They're difficult to miss," said Helen, smiling. And the colours *were* neon-like.

Stephan rose from his chair, simultaneously removing a large handkerchief from his pocket. He tied this handkerchief around his eyes, turning it into an improvised blindfold. "Check it, please," he said to me. I hesitated a moment, then rose, too. Stephan had done a good job of obscuring his vision. The handkerchief was tied tighter than I would have tied it.

Stephan struggled out of his jacket, and handed it to me. "Guide my hand to the bowl," he said. I did so, wondering what the chubby fellow had in mind. Everyone else in the jazz bar was now looking over at our table. Stephan caressed the top of the bowl, then turned his head dramatically away, so he was facing towards the piano. He then dipped his hand in among the Skittles and began, rapidly, to pull out all the blue ones, which he placed in a pile on the table. He then did the same with the yellow ones, then the green, then the red, then the orange, until finally there were only purple ones left. I've no idea how he did it.

"That's amazing," said Helen.

"Yes," said Stephan. "My fingers see." People in the bar applauded him as he removed his blindfold. "I am not a handsome man," he added, bowing slightly to them, "I know this. But I have my mystery. Thank you again for the drink, Charlie." He shuffled away again, taking his Spanish coffee into the back room.

"Well," I said. "That was pretty remarkable. —What's wrong?" There was a strange expression on Helen's face.

"How did he know your name?" asked Helen. "You never told him."

"God, I didn't, did I?" I said. "And you never called me by name?"

"I'm sure I didn't," said Helen. "That's pretty spooky." But she was smiling—the incident clearly lent a little more magic to the evening. And for my part, I was perfectly content to accept that there are things about the world we don't have to understand.

And so, after a couple more sets, we decided the night was over, and we also decided, wordlessly, that we would not complicate things by having one of us go home with the other. We sensed, I think—I'm sure—that there would be time enough for that. I paid the bill and we went outside, back onto Queen Street West, and I hailed a cab, and put her in it, trying without success to prepay the cabby. "No, no, no—don't take his money," Helen said, laughing. "Just drive away." So the cab driver drove off into the night, though Helen looked out the back window and blew me a kiss. My heart soared.

But I wasn't ready for bed myself, and I was still in the grip of my old teenage habit of walking, so I set out to walk further east along Queen Street West, enjoying the night air and the glimpses into scores of little restaurants and bistros and bars, to say nothing of the funky shops that lined the street, many of whose front windows were at least partially lit. And, of course, there were still people out, enjoying the same things I was enjoying, or simply going to or coming from work. Eventually, I reached Yonge Street, where, briefly, the number of people increased dramatically, but as I travelled further east the crowds fell away, and Queen Street East, which I'd never walked before late at night, revealed itself to be a shabbier, darker place than the west side I'd recently left. I was lighthearted, however, and my mind was filled with romantic possibilities, so I didn't register that the streetscape had become uncongenial for strolling until about twenty minutes after I'd crossed Yonge Street—at which point there was no other pedestrian in sight, and even the car traffic had diminished to almost none.

So there I was, sometime after midnight, on a dark stretch of Queen Street East, when suddenly I heard pounding steps behind me. I had just passed a cross street, and it was from that direction that the noise was coming, and within a moment or two the sound became much clearer because whoever it was had rounded the corner and was coming closer and closer to me. I turned and saw a large white man in his early twenties racing towards me, his right arm pumping and his left arm clutching something to his chest. I stepped to the side of the sidewalk, as close as I could to the storefronts, and this fellow rushed past me, his long, greasy hair flying behind him. But as he passed I saw what it was he was carrying—a tiny baby. And the child was crying piteously.

On such occasions we are compelled to make quick decisions. My first and most pressing desire was to do nothing. The man was bigger than I was, and wild-looking, and he hadn't challenged me in any way; additionally, I had consumed at least three beers over the course of the evening, so I wasn't in the best condition for an extended chase; finally, I was in the midst of deciding that I might be in love, and while I would have welcomed the opportunity to defend Helen from this or any other large male, she was not under threat. No, I didn't want to get involved.

But this fellow wasn't being pursued—not that I could see—and that suggested that the baby wasn't in any danger from someone else; and if the baby wasn't in any danger from someone else, that meant the baby might well be in danger from the runner himself, who was holding the child in a way that I thought very reckless. So, with a quick curse, I gave chase myself, shouting, "Wait! Stop! Let me talk to you!"

The runner did not pause—if anything he ran faster—but I had a couple of advantages, in spite of the beers in my system. He had been running for some distance, and I hadn't; and I had been walking for years and years, and my leg muscles were pretty well developed. It did not altogether surprise me, then, that over the course of the next two blocks I began to close the distance between us, and within another block I was only a few steps behind him, and he was beginning to flag.

As we approached another cross street the fellow suddenly deked left, taking himself and the baby under the overhang in front of a combination head shop and tattoo parlour. He whipped round to face me, raising his right arm in front of himself in the universal sign for halt. I halted.

"What the fuckin' hell do you want?" he said, gasping for air, yes, but coherent enough. His chest was heaving and his eyes were wild. The baby, who couldn't have weighed more than about twelve pounds, made a strange sound, and I wondered whether it might be suffering from whiplash.

"Is that your baby?" I asked.

The runner snarled at me—he literally bared his teeth. "Get away from me—get away," he said, beginning to back up. But in backing up he put himself against the locked door of the tattoo parlour, and suddenly he had nowhere else to go except through me.

"I don't want to hurt you," I said, as soothingly as I could manage. "I'm just worried about the baby. I'm worried that its neck may be hurt with all that flopping around."

"The fuckin' baby is fine," the runner said. His eyes were darting from side to side, trying to gauge his chances at getting clear of me.

"Is it your baby?" I asked again.

"Fuck off," he said.

I came to another decision: the baby could not be his—or in the almost impossible event that it was, *he* was in no state to look after it. I guessed that he was high on something—high to the point of psychosis. "Please give me the child," I said.

"Fuck off," he said, even more vehemently.

"Give me the child," I repeated.

"You wanna buy it?" he asked, focusing in on me for a moment. "Then you can do what you want with it. You got money?" He was sweating, and he stank of dope and dirt. A drop of sweat fell on the baby.

"Sure." I reached into the breast pocket of my jacket, removing my wallet. "Fifty bucks?" I said, checking the compartments.

"Everything you've fucking got," he said, beckoning with the fingers of his right hand and clutching the baby ever more tightly.

"That's all I have," I said—and I took the bills out of the wallet and held them out towards him.

The runner grabbed the money with his right hand, clumsily fanned the bills out, and then, in a move that caught me by surprise, threw the child at me, while simultaneously bolting to his left. I was able, thank God, to catch the baby, though its blanket fell to the ground. Of course, I had no interest in going after the kidnapper—as I assumed him to be. My priority was to get the child somewhere safe.

There were no taxis, and no other cars, on the street as I began to retrace my steps. I didn't run, for fear that running would further rattle the baby, and I tried, by talking soothingly, to reassure the child that she (for it was a she) was safe. She cried lustily for a block or two, then seemed to take some comfort from the rhythm of my walking and accepted the pacifier that I found tied to the zip on her sleeper. Her features were very delicate, and I guessed that she was Asian—though whether she was Thai or Vietnamese or Cambodian I could not be sure. I've never been good at distinguishing ethnicities.

We were halfway down the block in which I'd first begun to give chase, when a police car suddenly swung around the corner the runner had taken onto Queen Street. Its flashing light was operative, though the siren wasn't on. As soon as the driver saw me he screeched to a stop, almost climbing the curb. An instant later and two officers erupted from the car and came running towards me, both with their hands on their holsters.

"Stand right there!" shouted one of them.

I stopped, and a moment later the two of them were a couple of feet away.

"What are you doing with that baby?" said the second officer. He was young, maybe a little younger than me, and he looked very agitated.

"I've just taken her from someone," I said. "A guy who was running with her. I followed him."

"Is she all right?" asked the other officer—an older man. He was eyeing me dubiously, but he'd made no move to take out his gun.

"I think so," I said. "But she was crying quite a bit a minute ago. She seems to have calmed down."

"Describe the man who had him," said the first cop.

"Tall. Dishevelled. My height—maybe a little taller. Heavier than me. Long, stringy hair," I said. "He was heading east."

The two officers looked at each other. "Okay," said the older one. "Would you come with us, sir? We'll need a statement."

"Sure," I said. They put me in the back of the cruiser, and a moment later I was taking my first trip in police custody. The younger cop quickly got on the radio to his dispatcher.

The ride to the police station lasted no more than a couple of minutes, and it—the station—was smaller and quieter than I imagined it would be. Maybe that's because it was a sub-precinct of some kind—almost a hole-in-the wall operation. When we arrived, the older police officer helped me out of the cruiser, and he and the younger man followed close behind me as we approached the main door. The younger cop nipped ahead to open that, and we passed down a short hall before coming into a room with a front counter, beyond which there were several desks. I found myself blinking in the bright light. But I had no time to notice anything else because as soon as we entered, my attention was drawn to a knot of three people at one of the desks—another police officer facing our way, and an Asian couple. All three rose and looked at us, the Asians turning to do so, and then the couple came running towards us, the woman in the lead, her arms outstretched. And the woman ... the woman was Milly—as alive as any woman could be, and utterly focused on her baby.

That focus lasted, understandably, as long as it took to make sure that the little one was all right, but once Milly was reassured, she gave the baby to her husband and came over and embraced me. We stood for a long moment hugging each other close, and on this occasion both of us were crying: I was comforting her every bit as much as she was comforting me. The police officers, and the husband, initially assumed this was simply relief on Milly's part and sympathy on my own, but in short order the full truth came tumbling out—that we knew each other, and that we were from the same village, sort of, in Ontario. I shook hands with the husband, and he smiled and smiled and couldn't stop thanking me. The evening wasn't over, not by a long shot—I had a statement to make, and the police took Milly and her family off to hospital to have the baby checked for internal damage—but for me the action was over: what remained was reflection, a mental ordering of things, a coming to terms with an extraordinary event.

As a teacher, now, for twenty-something years, I've had the experience of imparting what I've hoped to be wise counsel to many a troubled student—but it's never the wise counsel they remember: it's the offhand comment, the throwaway line, the unguarded opinion. All too often, too, of course, it's what I *do* they remember, not what I *say*. And even more frequently, I suspect, they don't remember me at all: at best, I'm a bit player in their lives. Or maybe I painted a bit of scenery. Or maybe I just cleaned out the ashtrays backstage. I've only been of real importance to a handful of people: my son, my second wife, the daughter of a girlfriend between my wives, a young woman I saved from choking ... and Milly. Milly and her family.

Later that evening I learned how the baby, Sky, came to be kidnapped. Milly and her husband actually lived in Guelph, Ontario—a city to the west of Toronto—but they had been visiting his sister, an invalid, whose apartment was three or four blocks north of Queen Street, and of course they'd brought their new child with them. They'd put Sky down to sleep that night in a bedroom with a fire escape, and the kidnapper, whoever he was, had come up it, jimmied the window, and gone back down with the child. Milly had heard something, and had arrived in the bedroom just in time to see the kidnapper jumping off the bottom of the fire escape and taking off down the street with her baby.

So that's how it was that Milly re-entered my life, bringing with her a husband who is, even now, my best friend, and a child to whom I play a fond if somewhat bewildered godfather. And who could have predicted it? Who could ever have said that this is the way our lives would work out? I have another friend, Alan, who says that these events were a stunning coincidence—one of those things that must inevitably happen when one considers the billions of human interactions that take place every hour of every day. And it could be. I recognize that.

But there's another possibility, and it's one that I at least want to entertain. Maybe there is a kind of fearful symmetry in our lives. Maybe, just maybe, there's an underlying order to things; and maybe, just maybe, we sometimes catch a glimpse of that order—a peek at the warp and woof of karmic justice. Maybe, just maybe, there's a strange, wild, cosmic plan.

And maybe God does want us to work things out for ourselves.

"You're not paying attention," said the squat little man by the pool at my health club—just before the lightning hit.

Oh, but I'm trying. I'm trying really, really hard.

Acknowledgements

My warm thanks to the good people at Turnstone Press—Todd Besant, Sharon Caseburg, and my editor and midwife, Wayne Tefs.